The woods were dark and ominous. Jessic shivered. She wondered if there were bears out here. Or poisonous snakes. Or *wolves*. An owl hooted and Jessica jumped.

Taking a deep breath, Jessica picked up her pace. *Ouch!* she muttered as she whacked her knee against a big log standing upright in the path. Rubbing her knee, she looked at the piece of wood in horror. What was a freshly cut log doing in the middle of the forest?

The camp legend came back to her, and a chill raced up her spine. What if the woodsman really did haunt the forest? And what if he liked to chop up sixteen-year-old girls and use them for firewood? She knew Lacey probably just made up the story to keep them from sneaking out at night, but still . . .

Jessica breathed a sigh of relief as she caught sight of the fallen tree where she was supposed to meet Paul. She hoped he wouldn't be late.

Practically running through the clearing to the tree, Jessica hopped up on the trunk and waited. She swung her feet in the air casually, trying to pretend she wasn't afraid. Jessica knew it had to be just about midnight. Where was Paul?

Suddenly she saw a shadow moving.

"Paul?" Jessica called out. There was no response. The shadow moved toward her.

"Paul, this isn't funny!" Jessica cried loudly. No response.

Her hair standing on end, Jessica slid quickly off the trunk and began to run. After just a few moments she felt lost. She collapsed against a tree.

Suddenly strong arms circled her waist.

# SWEET VALLEY High®

# MEET ME AT MIDNIGHT

### Written by
### Kate William

### Created by
### FRANCINE PASCAL

BANTAM BOOKS
NEW YORK · TORONTO · LONDON · SYDNEY · AUCKLAND

RL 6, age 12 and up

MEET ME AT MIDNIGHT
*A Bantam Book / June 1996*

*Sweet Valley High*® *is a registered trademark of Francine Pascal*
*Conceived by Francine Pascal*
*Produced by Daniel Weiss Associates, Inc.*
*33 West 17th Street*
*New York, NY 10011*
*Cover art by Bruce Emmett*

ISBN: 0-553-56761-6

*Published simultaneously in the United States and Canada*

*Bantam Books are published by Bantam Books, a division of Bantam*
*Doubleday Dell Publishing Group, Inc. Its trademark, consisting of the*
*words "Bantam Books" and the portrayal of a rooster, is Registered in U.S.*
*Patent and Trademark Office and in other countries. Marca Registrada.*
*Bantam Books, 1540 Broadway, New York, New York 10036.*

PRINTED IN THE UNITED STATES OF AMERICA

OPM     0 9 8 7 6 5 4 3 2 1

*To Anita Elliott Anastasi*

# Chapter 1

"Liz! Are you surprised?" Todd Wilkins exclaimed on Monday afternoon at Camp Echo Mountain. He leaned against his black BMW in front of the main lodge, a self-satisfied grin spread across his face.

*Surprised?* sixteen-year-old Elizabeth Wakefield asked herself, staring at her boyfriend with a mixture of horror and shock. *Surprised is an understatement. Stunned is more like it.*

The last person Elizabeth had expected to see in the mountains of Montana was her longtime boyfriend from Sweet Valley, California. She had just been swimming in the lake with Joey Mason, the eighteen-year-old drama counselor with whom she'd gotten romantically involved at camp. Still dripping from their swim, she and Joey had walked hand in hand up to the main lodge. Then Elizabeth had received a double whammy. First she caught sight of Todd's BMW. Then she saw Todd himself. Elizabeth had dropped Joey's hand like a hot potato.

Elizabeth bit her lip and wrapped her beach towel around her body. She looked quickly from Todd to Joey. Should she introduce them? What could she say? *Joey, meet Todd, my boyfriend from home? Todd, meet Joey, my summer fling?* "Uh," she stammered nervously, her heart beating a drumroll in her chest.

But Todd didn't seem to notice her hesitation. Before she could get a word out, he pulled her toward him and enveloped her in a bear hug.

As Todd wrapped his arms around her Elizabeth glanced out of the corner of her eye at Joey. His handsome features creased in hurt and anger, and his green eyes clouded over. She gave him an imploring look, but he stared back at her impassively. Then he turned and strode away.

Todd lifted her face toward his and kissed her softly. He pulled her closer, cradling her head against his chest. "Oh, Liz," he murmured into her hair. "I've been dreaming about this moment for days."

"Me too," Elizabeth echoed, twisting to look at Joey's retreating figure. She felt suffocated in Todd's arms. She didn't know if it was the oppressive heat or the oppressive sensation of Todd's embrace that was making her feel dizzy. Her mind was spinning with a million questions. What was Todd doing here? He was supposed to be at basketball camp in California. Had he seen her and Joey holding hands? What was Joey going to think? She had told Joey that she and Todd were free to date other people. Now Joey would probably never speak to her again.

"Well, you two sure look cozy!" came a shout from the lodge.

Elizabeth pulled out of Todd's embrace and turned in the direction of the familiar, grating voice. It was Nicole Banes, Elizabeth's archrival at camp. Nicole was sitting in a rocking chair on the porch of the main lodge, swaying slowly back and forth. Her arms were folded across her chest, and a triumphant smirk was plastered on her face. It looked like she had caught the whole scene.

*Well,* Elizabeth thought with a sinking heart. *Out of the frying pan and into the fire.*

Nicole hopped out of the chair and skipped down the steps of the porch. Swinging her canteen of water over her shoulder, she marched up to them jauntily. Nicole was a tough-looking girl with short choppy hair. She was wearing cutoff jeans, a crew-neck white T-shirt, and sunglasses. A pair of worn brown hiking boots covered her feet and her signature red baseball cap was pulled down low on her forehead, twisted around backward as usual.

"Aren't you going to introduce us?" Nicole asked as she reached them.

Elizabeth took a deep breath and composed herself. "Todd, this is Nicole Banes," she said. "She's the waterskiing junior counselor here at camp."

Todd gave Nicole a friendly handshake. "It's nice to meet you, Nicole. I was hoping to have the chance to meet some of Elizabeth's friends at camp."

Nicole smiled sweetly. "Elizabeth and I have gotten to be really good friends."

*Archenemies is more like it,* Elizabeth thought.

Elizabeth's mouth dropped open as Nicole brazenly checked Todd out. Taking off her sunglasses, Nicole let her eyes wander slowly up and down Todd's body, from his wavy brown hair to his warm coffee-colored eyes to his muscular, athletic build.

"Elizabeth told us she had a boyfriend far away, but she didn't tell us how *hot* he was," Nicole said in appreciation.

Todd's face flushed pink.

"I guess she wanted to make sure none of us would move in on her territory," Nicole went on. "I mean, Eliz—" Suddenly Nicole let out a little cry and crumpled to the ground.

Todd jumped to her side. "What is it?"

"Oh, it's nothing," Nicole said, giving Todd a brave smile. "It's just my ankle. It goes out all the time. I think it's tendinitis or something."

Elizabeth rolled her eyes at Nicole's false act of bravado. Nicole's ankle never went out. She was out on the lake every day waterskiing, showing off her fancy jumps and flips. She obviously just wanted to get Todd's attention.

"Let me help you," Todd offered, kneeling by her side. "I'm a basketball player, and tendinitis is our number-one ailment." Todd was the star player of the Gladiators, the varsity basketball team at Sweet Valley High.

Elizabeth walked away, unable to bear the scene any longer. She leaned against a tree and watched in disgust while Todd tended to Nicole. She sighed. Just when things were beginning to get better, it looked like her world was about to crumble into pieces again.

This summer certainly hadn't turned out like she'd planned. When some of the students from Sweet Valley High had decided to work as junior counselors at Camp Echo Mountain for a month in the summer, Elizabeth had been wholly enthusiastic. Camp Echo Mountain was a performing arts camp with a renowned drama department, and Elizabeth had been hoping to write the play for the summer production.

She had been looking forward to the chance to hang out with some of her friends from Sweet Valley as well. Her twin sister, Jessica, who had high aspirations to become a famous actress, had jumped at the chance to attend the camp. Jessica had talked her best friend, Lila Fowler, into coming along with her. Aaron Dallas, the cocaptain of the soccer team at Sweet Valley High, and Winston Egbert, who was affectionately known as the class clown, had decided to act as junior counselors, too. Rich, snobby Lila Fowler wasn't exactly Elizabeth's type, but Aaron and Winston were always a lot of fun.

Then Elizabeth found out that one of her best friends from junior high, Maria Slater, was going to be at camp, too. When Maria had called her with the news, Elizabeth had been convinced that this was going to be the best summer ever. A former child actress, Maria had been assigned the position of assistant to the director. Elizabeth was thrilled. Not only would she and Maria get the opportunity to rekindle their friendship, they would also get the chance to work together on the camp play. Maria had been just as excited as Elizabeth. She couldn't wait to introduce

Elizabeth to her good friend Nicole. "You'll love her," Maria had enthused.

Instead Nicole Banes had turned out to be the bane of Elizabeth's existence. Elizabeth didn't know when she'd ever met a nastier, more two-faced girl. For the first time in her life Elizabeth had experienced hate at first sight. *It looks like the two of us are going to have our own little war,* Nicole had predicted one night. And she was right. Since they'd met, they'd been fighting for everything—the camp play, Maria's friendship, and Joey's love.

Elizabeth gritted her teeth as she recalled in her mind the girl's dirty stunts. Nicole had tried to steal Elizabeth's play. For a week straight Elizabeth had sneaked out at night in order to find the time to compose the camp play. But as soon as she had finished, Nicole had stolen Elizabeth's computer disk, claiming the script as her own. And Joey and Maria had believed Nicole. "Don't worry, Elizabeth," Joey had said when Elizabeth protested. "You can write the introduction to the play." Elizabeth's face flamed at the memory.

*It wasn't enough that Nicole stole my work,* Elizabeth thought bitterly. *She stole my friends, too!* She had bad-mouthed Elizabeth to both Maria and Joey. Maria and Elizabeth's friendship had fallen apart, and Joey had started dating Nicole.

But everything had worked out. Jessica had found an incriminating video and had proved the play was Elizabeth's. Elizabeth's good name had been restored, and she had received the credit she deserved. Both Joey and Maria had realized what a snake

Nicole really was. Elizabeth and Maria had made up, and most important, Elizabeth and Joey had finally gotten together.

But now that Todd had unexpectedly shown up, anything could happen. Elizabeth's stomach twisted nervously as she watched Todd rubbing Nicole's ankle. She was sure Nicole would find some way to turn the situation to her advantage.

"That should do it," Todd announced. He fished a blue bandanna out of his backpack and wrapped it expertly around Nicole's ankle, tucking in the corner to secure it.

"Oh, thanks, Todd, it's much better," Nicole cooed, wriggling her ankle and batting her eyelashes. She jumped up and tested her weight on the foot.

"Anytime." Todd grinned, standing up and coming over to the tree where Elizabeth was waiting. Nicole followed quickly behind, walking with a pronounced limp.

"Any part of you that needs fixing?" Todd asked Elizabeth, wrapping an arm around her waist.

"I'm fine," Elizabeth said stiffly, resisting the urge to push his hand away.

"So, you're Elizabeth's boyfriend?" Nicole asked.

*Brilliant deduction,* Elizabeth thought wryly.

"Elizabeth's longtime steady boyfriend," Todd agreed.

"I really admire couples with long-term romances," Nicole said. "I think loyalty's the most important thing in a relationship. It's all a matter of trust. Don't you agree, Elizabeth?"

Elizabeth nodded, her face burning.

"A relationship without trust is no relationship at all," Todd put in.

"My sentiments exactly!" Nicole agreed. "It's so refreshing to see such a stable couple."

Elizabeth shifted her feet nervously.

"You know, a lot of kids would be worried to be separated for a whole month," Nicole added.

Elizabeth tugged on Todd's arm. She didn't know how much more she could take of Nicole's game. But Todd didn't notice. He seemed engrossed by Nicole's words.

Nicole went on. "I mean, it's tough for even the most dedicated couples. You come to camp and suddenly your significant other seems light-years away. And you're surrounded by lots of hot junior counselors." She smiled at Elizabeth. "Not to mention *senior* counselors."

Elizabeth began to panic. She had to get Todd out of there before Nicole got to the punch line of her joke. "Todd, I'm feeling a little faint. Do you think we can walk down to the water where it's cooler?"

Nicole's eyes twinkled. "Well, I hope we'll be seeing *a lot* of you!" she said to Todd, a big friendly smile spread across her face. Then her eyes lit up, as if she were suddenly struck by an idea. "And you know what? In honor of your visit, I think you should expect a surprise at dinner." She winked at Todd. Now Elizabeth really thought she was going to pass out.

"What a great girl!" Todd said enthusiastically as they walked toward the lake.

Elizabeth sighed. She felt like she had walked

8

into a bad dream. And she had an uncanny feeling that the nightmare had just begun.

"Summer love is sweet but cruel," Jessica Wakefield intoned dramatically, walking the length of the female junior counselors' cabin. "As fleeting as the light of a firefly."

Jessica was rehearsing her lines for the drama auditions, which were to be held later that afternoon. The play was called *Lakeside Love,* and Jessica was trying out for the female lead.

Jessica repeated the lines of her monologue out loud, glad to have a few moments to herself to practice. Usually the cabin was full of chattering girls.

Jessica crinkled her nose as she surveyed the sparse room where the six female junior counselors were housed. The cabin had slatted wood walls and tiny windows covered with shabby red-and-white-gingham flowered curtains. There were six bunks, four on one side and two on the other. Cheap plywood dressers were squeezed in between the beds, and a rickety wooden desk stood under the window at the far end of the cabin.

*Not only is this place horribly cramped, but it's unbearably tacky.* Lila had almost fainted when she caught sight of the cabin. Jessica smiled at the memory of her friend's shocked expression. For Lila, roughing it meant staying in a bed-and-breakfast instead of a five-star hotel. Jessica cocked her head to one side, mentally redoing the room. With some new curtains and a few posters on the wall, it could have a sort of rustic homey feel.

9

Then Jessica shook her head. Now wasn't the time to be redecorating the cabin. She had serious work to do. Play tryouts were in just a few hours.

Jessica walked down the narrow aisle and continued with her monologue. "But better to have loved and lost than never to have loved at all," she recited, her voice ringing out in the empty room. Then she stopped, confused. That wasn't the play.

Jessica fell back onto her bunk and picked up the script, studying her lines. Staring up at the peaked ceiling, she let herself drift into another time and place. She was Alexandra, the beautiful and willful female lead in the play. She was at a camp just like this one, but in a time long ago. Jessica went over the plot in her head, trying to make it as real as possible.

Elizabeth had written a variation of the camp legend. The play centered on the secret love affair between Alexandra, the head counselor at Camp Echo Mountain, and a woodsman who did odd jobs at the camp. When their affair was exposed, the owner of the camp banished the woodsman forever.

Faced with the loss of her one true love, the head counselor had an impossible decision to make. She could give up her whole life to follow him or remain apart from him forever. After an agonizing separation, she ran into the forest to find him. They disappeared into the woods together, never to be seen again.

Even though the lovers were gone, their memories remained alive. The ghosts of the characters haunted the camp, creating a legend that was told and retold for generations to come. The play closed with a black stage and the eerie sound of chopping wood.

Jessica fully identified with the main character. Just like Alexandra, Jessica was daring and reckless and spontaneous. She, too, would take risks to get what she wanted. Closing her eyes, Jessica felt herself becoming Alexandra. She saw herself running impetuously into the tangled woods, falling into the handsome woodsman's arms, and disappearing with him under the cover of night. And then becoming a legend herself.

Standing up, Jessica went to the center of the room and struck a dramatic pose. She swept her blond hair on top of her head and put a regal expression on her face. "If this is my destiny, I will bear it with grace and dignity. For our love, I will shed no tears."

Then Jessica jumped to the end of the monologue, shifting moods rapidly. She marched to the window and gazed out at the woods, picturing a dark sky and a full red moon. She clenched her fist around the windowsill and raised her voice in anguish. "In the flicker of an instant, my fate will be sealed. Why should someone so young be forced to grow up so quickly? With so little life behind me, how can I decide upon my proper path?"

Finally her face took on an expression of calm, and her voice dropped to almost a whisper. "But I am not choosing my fate. It has chosen me." Jessica closed her eyes and let her voice catch. A tear came to her eye and trickled down her cheek. She fell back against the wall, a martyred expression on her face.

A moment later Jessica dropped out of character and bowed to the audience, envisioning loud applause and a chorus of "Bravos!" She jumped aside as a bouquet of long-stemmed roses landed on the stage.

Smiling at her own imagination, Jessica flopped down on her bunk on her stomach. She was exhausted. She had been practicing for hours, and she knew her lines inside out. "Summer love is sweet but cruel," she said aloud. "Summer love . . . ," she repeated. Her voice trailed off as her thoughts drifted away from Alexandra and the woodsman to herself and Paul Mathis.

Paul Mathis was a gorgeous local with whom Jessica had fallen in love. Paul was the older brother of Tanya, one of Jessica's campers. He lived with his parents, who owned a popular diner in town.

At the start of camp Jessica had resolved to have a romance-free summer. She had recently been through too many traumas in the love department, and she had decided that she needed to be alone in order to recover.

Propping her chin up on her hands, Jessica went over the events of the past few months. It had all started when she had decided to learn to surf. At first her interest in surfing was motivated solely by the desire to win a surfing contest and a trip to Hawaii. But then she had developed a real passion for the sport—and for her surfing teacher, Christian Gorman.

Jessica had met Christian her first day out on the water. For a month they spent every morning together, riding the waves of the foamy Pacific Ocean.

They had a secret affair that eventually destroyed Jessica's relationship with her boyfriend, Ken Matthews. Then Christian had been killed in a tragic accident. First Jessica had lost Ken, and then she had lost Christian. It had been too much for her, and Jessica had decided to have a boyless summer.

But the moment Paul Mathis stepped out of his muddy red pickup truck, Jessica's resolve melted into thin air. The first time she saw him, he was wearing jeans and a faded plaid flannel shirt with the sleeves cut off. Jessica found his rugged good looks irresistible. He had wavy black hair and dark, smoldering eyes that glimmered with a silver light.

At their first meeting sparks had flown between them. Paul had come to the camp to pick up his sister to take her to their grandmother's birthday party. Tanya, who idolized Jessica, had washed her hair in peroxide to become a blonde, too. When Paul had gotten a look at his sister, he had practically exploded. "Who gave you the crazy idea to turn yourself into a dumb blonde?" he had railed.

"Watch what you say about blondes," Jessica had returned angrily.

And that was the start of a fiery romance. After that exchange, Jessica couldn't get Paul Mathis out of her mind. And it turned out that Paul couldn't get Jessica out of his mind, either. When Tanya reported that Paul had asked about her nonstop all weekend, Jessica decided to pay him a visit.

The only problem was that she didn't have a car. But Jessica didn't let that stop her. Lacey Cavannah, the owner of the camp, had lent Jessica her Ford

Bronco to do a few errands for her in town. Since she still had the keys, Jessica thought she should make use of them.

So last night Jessica had "borrowed" the camp owner's car and headed for the diner in town that Paul's parents owned. But her second meeting with Paul was no different from the first. They had fought and Jessica stormed off in a huff.

Then she got a flat tire on her way back to camp and Paul had shown up. He changed the tire for her, as well as giving her a heart-stopping kiss. Her lips were still tingling from it.

*Lila thinks a romance-free summer is a bad idea,* Jessica mused. "The best way to get over one guy is to find another," she had said. *Maybe Lila's right.* Maybe jumping into a new romance *was* the best way to get over Christian.

But there was no way she was going to let Lila have the satisfaction of seeing her cave. Jessica made a new resolve. She was going to get Paul Mathis. And it was going to be top secret.

"This is Lake Vermillion," Elizabeth explained as she and Todd walked down to the water's edge. A huge mountain rose out behind the lake, and the blue-green water sparkled in the late afternoon sun. A few sailboats rocked lazily on the horizon and colorful windsurfers drifted by. Even though she was out sailing on the water every day, Elizabeth was always struck afresh by the quiet beauty of the lakefront.

"The lake looks like a big lima bean," Todd remarked.

Elizabeth's stomach lurched as she looked out at the oval-shaped lake, where she and Joey had been swimming just moments before. She could see Joey's strong body cutting a smooth line across the water as he raced her toward the shore. And she could see his rakish smile and crinkling green eyes as he climbed out of the water and took her hand. Then she shook her head hard, trying to shake away the vivid image. Elizabeth threw her towel on the grass and plopped down on it.

"The activities cabins are on this side of the lake," Elizabeth said, speaking quickly to hide her anxiety. She indicated a cluster of small wooden cabins that were peeking through the trees. "Each counselor is in charge of a workshop, and most of them are held in the cabins. I'm the sailing junior counselor, so I spend most of my time here, in the boathouse and on the dock. Rose is the name of my senior counselor." Elizabeth twisted around to her right and pointed to a massive log cabin with three stone chimneys. "That big building is the main lodge. The mess hall and the kitchen are in there."

Elizabeth paused for breath, feeling like a flight attendant. Her own voice sounded foreign to her ears. She realized she was babbling on and on about the camp, but she couldn't help herself. She was nervous and wanted to keep Todd from discussing anything personal.

"That's the nature cabin," Elizabeth continued, her voice tight and thin. "That's the drama cabin, that's the tumbling cabin—"

Todd gave her an odd look. "Elizabeth, are you OK?" he asked.

15

"Of course," Elizabeth responded. "I'm just so excited to see you." She forced a bright smile and took a shaky breath.

Todd smiled at her and gave her a kiss. Then he pulled back and looked at her with a mischievous glint in his brown eyes. "Where's your cabin?" he asked. "Just in case I decide to make a late night visit."

Elizabeth ignored the insinuation. "The girls' cabins are on that side of the lake," she said, pointing to a cluster of small wooden cabins to the right. "And on the other side of the lake are the boys' cabins."

Todd grinned. "Well, that's good. At least I don't have to worry about any nighttime raids from the guys."

Elizabeth smiled weakly, thinking about the raid on Saturday night that Joey had led. Dressed in ghost costumes, the guys had sneaked across Lake Vermillion in canoes and crashed at the girls' campfire.

"What's that?" Todd asked, pointing to a quaint little white house that stood in the shadows of the main lodge.

"That's the camp office and Lacey Cavannah's house," Elizabeth explained.

"Who's Lacey?" Todd asked.

"She's the woman who owns the camp. She's a widowed southerner. I think summer camp is like a surrogate family for her." Elizabeth smiled wryly, thinking of her unfortunate encounters with Lacey. "Or maybe a penal colony. She runs this place with an iron fist."

Elizabeth hadn't exactly made a good impression

16

on the camp owner. Not only was Elizabeth doing a terrible job as the sailing junior counselor, but her campers had absolutely no respect for her. The first day of camp one of the campers had nicknamed her "Dizzy Lizzie" and the name had stuck. "Why can't you be more like your sister?" Lacey had complained one day. "Hardworking, sensible, honest." Elizabeth had wanted to scream. *She* was the responsible one in the family. Jessica was notorious for her fun-loving, scheming ways.

Elizabeth shook her head. Her sister had really pulled one over on Lacey. The camp owner would blow her top if she knew that Jessica had sneaked into town the night before in Lacey's Bronco.

"Lacey's not nice at all?" Todd asked.

"I guess that depends on if she likes you or not," Elizabeth replied. "If you do a good job, Lacey can be the warmest woman around. But if you mess up—" Elizabeth slid a finger across her throat. "The JCs have a lot of responsibilities, and Lacey makes sure they all get done properly," she explained. "All the JCs run a workshop and are in charge of a group of assigned campers. They also have to perform at least one KP duty a day and—"

"Whoa! Wait a minute!" Todd interrupted, holding up a hand and laughing. "JC? KP? Is there a secret language for this camp?"

Elizabeth smiled apologetically. "Oh, sorry. I guess I've gotten so used to the lingo here that I don't even notice I'm using it. JC stands for junior counselor, and KP means kitchen patrol—a food-serving or cleanup duty."

Todd made a face. "This is beginning to sound like boot camp."

Elizabeth laughed. "Sometimes I think it is. Especially when my monstrous group of ten-year-olds force me to act like an army sergeant. Jessica got really lucky. She's the dance JC, and she's in charge of the youngest campers at camp, an adorable group of seven- and eight-year-olds. In fact, her campers are so infatuated with her that they imitate her every move. They dress like her, they walk like her, and they talk like her. Jessica made up a name for them— Wannabees."

Elizabeth stopped for breath and looked at Todd. He was staring at her intently, but he didn't seem to be taking in what she was saying.

"Todd, have you heard a word that I've said?" she reprimanded him.

"Of course," Todd responded. "You were talking about Wannabees. And I *wannabee* in your arms." Todd grinned sheepishly at his bad pun, then quickly pulled her toward him and wrapped his arms around her.

"Oh, Liz, I've missed you so much," he whispered in her ear. "Being away made me realize how much I love you. As soon as I got a break from basketball camp I packed up my car and headed to Montana to see you."

Elizabeth felt like a horrible person, but she couldn't help aching for Joey. She thought of their kiss by the lake earlier that morning. She and Joey had taken a swim out to the dock in the middle of the lake. As they lay drying in the sun Joey had leaned over and given her a delicious, sun-warmed kiss. Moments later he had dropped a handful of cold water on her bare belly. Shocked by the blast of cold, Elizabeth had retaliated by shoving him off the dock. Then she had dived in after him, and they had raced to the shore. Elizabeth's pulse quickened as she remembered the playful, romantic scene.

Suddenly it struck her why she was longing to be with Joey. With Joey, she felt energized. She felt one hundred percent alive. Elizabeth looked at Todd carefully. For the first time in her life Elizabeth saw her longtime boyfriend as Jessica did—as boring-as-butter Todd Wilkins.

*Actually*, Elizabeth mused, *Todd has much better qualities than Joey*. Todd was steady and dependable, and Joey was wild and unpredictable. Todd made her feel secure, and Joey made her feel nervous and vulnerable.

But Elizabeth didn't feel like being safe anymore. She was sick of being solid and reliable Elizabeth Wakefield. She wanted some excitement—she wanted to be with Joey. She had to get Todd out of here. And fast.

"Todd, you shouldn't have come here," Elizabeth asserted, twisting around to face him.

Todd looked wounded. "Aren't you glad to see me?"

"Of course, I'm thrilled that you came," Elizabeth said, trying not to let the annoyance she was feeling creep into her voice. "But Lacey is very strict. I could lose my job."

Todd laughed. "Well, I've got another surprise for you."

19

Elizabeth groaned. She didn't think she could handle any more surprises.

"I called ahead and got special visiting privileges. I can stay in Winston's cabin." Todd beamed at her. "Isn't that great?"

Elizabeth's heart sank and she gave him a thin smile. It looked like she'd really gotten herself into a mess.

"But I am not choosing my fate. It has chosen me," Jessica finished, her voice ringing out strong and clear in the auditorium. She paused dramatically, then bowed her head slightly. There was a hush in the audience, and then quiet applause followed.

Jessica was on the wooden stage of the drama cabin, giving her reading for tryouts. Maggie, one of Jessica's campers, was taping the auditions with the video camera she had brought to camp. Maggie was a freckled-faced girl with matted brown pigtails. Tanya was helping her out with the camera.

"Great!" Joey said, clapping from the audience, where about forty kids were gathered in the wooden seats. "Everybody take a break. We'll assign roles in about fifteen minutes."

Jessica flashed Joey a smile and he grinned back. She could see why Elizabeth was interested in him. Joey was tall and muscular, with eyes the color of green leaves and light curly brown hair that hung low over his forehead. He had an easy way about him. He was wearing cutoff navy blue sweatpants and a faded yellow T-shirt, and a three-day growth of stubble darkened his strong jaw.

In Jessica's opinion Joey Mason was the direct opposite of boring-as-butter Todd Wilkins. Even though her sister wouldn't admit anything, Jessica was sure something was going on between Joey and Elizabeth. Elizabeth's knees got all wobbly at the sight of him, and she tended to lose her powers of speech in his presence. Jessica smiled to herself. Sometimes Elizabeth surprised her. It was good to see her perfect sister acting like the bad twin for a change.

"Joey! Joey!" Maggie cried, running after him as he walked across the stage. "Don't forget the tape!"

Joey turned around, and Maggie barreled into him. "Whoa!" Joey laughed, untangling the girl from his long legs. He crouched down to her level.

"What have you got?" he asked.

Maggie popped the tape out of the video camera and handed it to him proudly. "I got the entire audition on tape!"

"Thanks, Maggie," Joey said, taking the cassette from her eagerly outstretched hand. "We'll need this to make important casting decisions." Maggie's eyes lit up with delight.

Joey stood up and walked to his office at the far end of the stage. Maggie ran eagerly by his side. "Do you want to be our assistant cameraman?" Joey offered.

"I want to be the assistant camerawoman!" Maggie yelled out.

Joey laughed and ruffled her hair.

Jessica laughed as well. She had to hand it to her. The girl had a feminist consciousness at the age of seven.

Jessica grabbed a lemonade from the refreshment table and sat on a prop on the stage. She was still flushed from her performance. She thought she gave a really inspired reading, and she was dying to get the lead in the play. Camp Echo Mountain had been the launching pad for a number of famous Hollywood stars. Jessica was determined to join their ranks, and she was sure the lead in the summer production would be an important step in that direction.

But she was faced with some stiff competition. There had been a big turnout for the tryouts. A number of JCs had auditioned for parts—Aaron from Sweet Valley; Justin Siena, a cute guy from Fresno, California; Buford and Johansen, a couple of sweet—if socially inept—guys from Pittsburgh; and Angela Davis, a pretty, dark-haired Spanish girl from New York. Jessica was a little worried about Angela. She had given a powerful, dramatic reading for Alexandra's part.

Most of the campers had shown up as well. A lot of little kids had tried out for minor roles, and almost all the older campers had auditioned for major parts. Jessica recognized some of the girls from Elizabeth's group of ten-year-olds—Aimee, a sturdy girl with mousy brown hair; Helen, a pale girl whose little face was hidden behind oversize round tortoiseshell glasses; and Adrienne, a radical-looking girl with close-cropped brown hair and three silver studs in her left ear. Aimee and Helen were huddled together, and they seemed to be *oohing* and *ahhing* over the script.

Lila's entire group of thirteen-year-olds had auditioned as well. They were lounging on the stage next to her, and Jessica could overhear their conversation.

"It's not fair that the JCs get to try out for parts," a tall, skinny blonde with long eyelashes complained. Her name was Tiffany and she had an obnoxious personality. She planned to go to New York to become a supermodel as soon as she got her braces off.

"I know," her best friend, Amber, agreed with a flip of her strawberry blond hair. "I mean, this is *our* camp, not theirs." Amber was a pudgy girl with porcelain skin and clear blue eyes.

Just then two little girls raced by on the stage.

"You're it!" one of them cried, tagging her friend.

"I am not!" yelled the other. "You didn't get me!"

"Ugh," Tiffany said with a look of disdain. "I really hope we're going to have separate rehearsals. It will be simply unbearable if all these little brats are running around."

Jessica smiled. No wonder Lila called her group the Sulky Six. They complained about everything. According to Lila, the thirteen-year-olds thought they were too mature for all the camp activities. "How childish" was their favorite refrain. The only workshop they liked to attend was waterskiing. *How perfect,* Jessica thought. *Of course the only counselor the Sulky Six like is nasty Nicole.* But Jessica had to agree with the girls' complaint about the younger campers. As cute as they were, she was glad that most of her campers hadn't auditioned for the play. She wouldn't get a moment's peace if the Wannabees were there. The only kids from her group who had auditioned were Maggie and Tanya, and they had been busy with the video camera.

Jessica stole a look at the far end of the stage, hoping her campers were still occupied. They were sitting together on the floor, quietly watching while Joey conferred with Maria Slater, his drama JC. It looked like Joey and Maria were making some important casting decisions. Joey pointed to the tape and said something. But Maria shook her head, rewinding the tape and gesticulating wildly.

Jessica looked at the tall black girl in admiration. Maria had been a film and commercial actress until she hit puberty. Then her family moved to Sweet Valley, and Maria vowed to be a "normal" American teenager. She and Elizabeth had become close friends. When Maria's family moved to New York City, Elizabeth had been crushed.

*But no matter what, Maria will never be normal,* Jessica thought. She was striking, with short dark hair and strong features. Even though she wasn't an actress anymore, she still had presence, a star quality about her.

Joey stood up and clapped. "OK, I think we've made our decisions," he announced. "Everybody gather round."

Jessica felt her mouth go dry as she took a seat on the floor. Within minutes everybody was sitting in a circle on the stage.

"Now, I'm going to go through the casting of all the major and minor parts," Joey said. "If your name's not called, don't worry. We still need you. Those not cast as actors will be part of the stage crew. And we'll always be able to use extras."

Jessica squirmed impatiently as he went through

24

the roles. "Campers in the mess hall: Jennifer, Aimee, Rupert, Ashley, Emily, Tanya, Maggie, and Tad. Ashley and Emily, you're senior counselors. Jennifer, you're the cook. Campers around the campfire: Tiffany, Amber, Samantha, Odette, Jamie, and Albert. Villagers: Buford, Johansen, Davis, Marissa, Jeffrey . . ." Jessica tuned him out as he listed the names. It seemed like there were a million minor parts.

Finally he got to the major roles. Jessica held her breath as he announced them. "The camp owner will be Angela Davis. For the woodsman part we've chosen our tumbling pro, Derek Sandler. And the female lead is—Jessica Wakefield."

Jessica let her breath out in a rush. She couldn't believe it. She had really done it. She had landed the lead role in the summer production.

"Nice going, Jessica," Angela said good-naturedly, patting her on the back.

"Thanks, Angela." Jessica smiled. She beamed with pleasure while everybody congratulated her.

Derek sidled up to her and slung an arm around her shoulders. "Hey, Jessica, we better start getting warmed up for our summer romance. How about tonight at the campfire?"

"Derek, I think we better leave all practicing for play rehearsal," Jessica said, lifting his arm off her shoulders.

"Ouch!" Derek said, making a pouty face.

Jessica was thrilled to have the lead role, but she wasn't thrilled to be starring opposite Derek Sandler. Jessica was working alone at the dance workshop, so Derek had been coming by to help out. He was a tall, muscular guy with an unnerving resemblance to Ken. Just like Ken, Derek had all-American good looks, sandy blond hair, and clear blue eyes. And he clearly had a crush on her.

But Jessica wasn't interested in Derek. The pain of her breakup with Ken was still too fresh in her mind. Jessica always felt a pang in her heart when she caught sight of Derek. Even though her relationship with Ken hadn't worked out, he'd been a good friend to her since childhood, and she didn't need to be reminded of how much she'd hurt him.

"The play will be held a week from Wednesday," Joey informed them. "That gives us a week and a half to get this production in tip-top shape. We will have play practice every afternoon after workshops."

"Lots of important casting agents will be at the performance," Maria added. "So put your all into it."

"Remember," Joey said. "Only ten percent of acting is talent . . ."

"And ninety percent is hard work!" Maria finished with a smile.

Jessica was prepared to work hard. She was determined to put on her best performance ever. And to make sure Paul Mathis saw it. Jessica was sure that if Paul saw her act, there would be no way he could help falling head over heels in love with her.

# Chapter 2

Jessica flew into the cabin before dinner, flushed with the success of her audition. She might have been through a hard time in the past few months, but she was over it now. The old Jessica Wakefield was back, the Jessica Wakefield who got what she wanted.

Jessica took a quick look in the mirror. Since she'd decreed a boyless summer, she'd been ignoring her appearance. But no more. She cocked her head and studied her reflection. What she needed was a face mask.

Jessica fished around in Lila's designer cosmetic bag and pulled out a jar of green facial cleaner. If she wanted to win Paul over and put on a showstopping performance, then she couldn't neglect her looks. And beauty started with the skin.

Jessica grabbed the jar and went to the mirror. Wrapping her hair up on her head in a knot, she dipped two fingers in the jar and began spreading the green paste evenly across her face. Her thoughts returned to Paul. Somehow he had really gotten under her skin. She couldn't believe she hadn't heard from him yet. She had been sure she would get a letter at lunch, but when Lacey had gone through mail call, Jessica's name hadn't been on the list.

Suddenly the door opened. Jessica turned. It was Lila, looking particularly cool and chic in a short tan linen skirt and a raw-silk T-shirt.

"Ack!" Lila screamed.

Jessica jumped, startled. "Lila, you scared me!"

"I scared *you*? How do you think *I* feel? I've just had an encounter with the green-faced ghoul."

Then Lila looked closer and picked up the jar off Jessica's bunk. "Hey! That's my Italian face mask!" She put her hands on her hips and mimicked Jessica. "Remember, Lila, we're going to *camp*, not a beauty spa."

While Lila was packing her bags to go to camp, she had accused Jessica of acting as the fashion police. Lila had crammed her suitcase full of extravagant items, from beaded evening gowns to silk suits. But Jessica had removed each piece of clothing just as quickly as Lila added it.

"Facial care has nothing to do with beauty," Jessica protested. "It has to do with *health*."

Lila wasn't convinced. "The only time you put on a face mask is when you've fallen for somebody. Which is exactly what you should do"—she looked at Jessica closely—"*if* you haven't done so already."

"That's ridiculous," Jessica scoffed. "I'm not interested in boys. *I* am recovering." She turned back to

28

the mirror and applied the mask to her forehead.

"I'm telling you, Jessica, love is the solution to everything," Lila said.

Jessica sighed. Lila had fallen in love with a JC named Beauregard the first day at camp. His nickname was Bo, and Lila had repeated his name endlessly in the last week. In fact, all of Lila's conversations seemed to be limited to the topic of Bo. All she seemed to say was "Bo this, Bo that." Jessica shook her head. Love had definitely turned Lila into a sentimental fool.

"I just can't get over it," Lila said, sauntering around the cabin. "I mean, I thought Beauregard was this outdoorsy mountain man. And it turns out that he comes from old money and enjoys the, ah, finer things in life."

Jessica sighed again. She'd heard this story about a hundred times. When Lila had first met Bo, he had acted like a granola type who loved nature and the wilderness. And so Lila had acted the same way. She had recounted Jessica's adventure in the desert of Death Valley as if it were her own. Then finally one night Bo confessed. His name was actually Beauregard Creighton III, and he came from a wealthy D.C. family—and he *loathed* the outdoors.

"Beauregard is *so* cultivated," Lila swooned. "Did I tell you that his mother is French and that her family owns vineyards in the Bordeaux region of France?"

Jessica rolled her eyes. "No, but you did tell me that his mother goes to Paris twice a year to attend the spring and fall fashion shows," she said in a snide voice.

Lila didn't seem to notice her tone. "Yes, that's right," she said. She paused at a bunk, striking a pose and resting her palm softly on the mattress. "Maybe she'll take me with her for the Armani show in the fall."

"I wish she'd take you with her now," Jessica muttered under her breath.

"Did you know that *beau* means 'beautiful' in French?" Lila laughed softly. "And to think I thought he was the outdoor type." Lila sighed. "Beauregard really is just the ideal man. Rough on the outside and sophisticated on the inside."

Jessica gritted her teeth. If she heard one more word about Beauregard Creighton III, she was going to scream.

Lila fumbled through her cosmetic bag and pulled out a stick of ruby red lipstick. "Well, I just came back to freshen up for a minute," she said. She pursed her lips into a cupid's bow and painted them expertly. After blotting her lips on a tissue, she gave Jessica a radiant smile. "Beauregard and I are going to having a little gourmet snack on the dock this week. We're having it sent express mail from the Gourmet Grocery in Sweet Valley."

Jessica shook her head. Sometimes Lila was just too much. Express mail to camp!

Lila grabbed her bag and turned to leave. But she stopped with her hand on the doorknob. "Oh, I almost forgot. I got a letter addressed to you at mail call today." She pulled an envelope out of her bag. "It must have gotten mixed up in my mail."

"A letter?" Jessica said excitedly, practically diving

on it. Her sixth sense told her it was from Paul.

Lila smiled, waving the envelope in the air out of Jessica's reach.

"Lila! Give me that!" Jessica said, swiping at it.

"What is it?" Lila asked, jumping up on her bunk and eyeing the envelope.

Jessica crossed her arms across her chest and tapped a foot impatiently. "It's a letter, Lila."

"Oh! So *that's* what it is," Lila said. She turned mischievous eyes to Jessica. "I wonder who it's from?" She held the envelope up to the light and tried to make out its contents.

"It's probably just from my parents," Jessica said.

"Hmm, I've never seen you so excited about a letter from home." Lila turned the envelope over. "I don't see a return address."

"That's because I know where they live," Jessica said dryly.

Lila smirked. "I thought you were going to have a romance-free summer."

"I *am* having a romance-free summer," Jessica insisted.

"Epistolary romances count as well," Lila pointed out.

"A what romances?" Jessica asked, rolling her eyes. Ever since Lila had started seeing Bo, she had become even more impossibly snobbish than usual. She had gotten into the habit of sprinkling her language with words Jessica had never heard before.

Lila stared at her in shock. "You don't know what an epistolary romance is?"

"No, and I bet you didn't either before you met Bo," Jessica replied in exasperation.

"An epistolary romance is a relationship of letters,"

31

Lila explained in a know-it-all tone. "Haven't you ever heard of the French book *Dangerous Liaisons*? If you want, you can read it when I'm done. Beauregard lent it to me. It's an eighteenth-century French novel written in the form of letters."

Jessica was getting fed up. She had no interest in eighteenth-century French books. Right now she was only interested in one twentieth-century letter.

She put her hands on her hips. "Lila Fowler! If you don't let go of that letter, I'm going to set all of my seven-year-old campers on you."

"Oh, no! A fate worse than death!" Lila cried. "An attack of the miniature Wannabees!" She pretended to be assaulted and fell flat onto the bed. Jessica couldn't help smiling at her out-of-character clowning. Lila's relationship with Bo was actually making Lila *goofy*.

Moments later she hopped off the bunk. Lila grabbed her bag off the bunk and flipped her mane of light brown hair over her shoulder. "See you later!" she said. She dropped the letter on the bed and floated out.

After Lila was gone, Jessica ripped open the envelope. At last she had gotten word from Paul. She was sure he'd suggest they meet again that night.

Then with a sinking heart she read his hastily scrawled note.

> Dear Jessica,
> Please don't try to see me again. I'm not interested in silly blondes with nothing between their ears.
>
> Paul

Jessica couldn't believe her eyes and read the note again. Her face burned with hurt and anger. She crumpled the note and threw it in the trash. *Silly blonde!* How *dare* he treat her this way?

Jessica went to the sink and washed the mask off her face furiously. Now she was more determined than ever to win Paul. Nobody rejected Jessica Wakefield. *Nobody*.

*Shoot! She's not here,* Elizabeth thought as she entered the mess hall on Monday evening. She had gotten to the dining room early, hoping to find Jessica, who was supposed to be on KP duty. If anyone would know how she could get out of her current mess, it would be her twin sister, queen of the schemers.

Elizabeth sat down on a bench in the corner and rested her head in her hands, feeling completely dejected. Soon dinner would start and she would be assaulted by her obnoxious campers—and Nicole's "surprise."

Then Jessica entered the dining hall, a row of Wannabees following her single file like little chicks. Elizabeth couldn't resist a smile as she watched the campers swing their hips Jessica Wakefield style. They were all wearing cutoff faded jean shorts and most of them had on T-shirts in shades of purple, Jessica's favorite color. And even though they were indoors, they were all sporting trendy cat-shaped sunglasses.

Elizabeth felt a twinge of jealousy. Unlike her ill-tempered ten-year-olds, Jessica had an adorable

33

group of seven- and eight-year-olds. Tanya, a cute girl with brown pigtails, was in the lead. Sofia, an angelic-looking little girl with saucerlike brown eyes and dark corkscrew curls, followed next in line. Her sister, Anastasia, walked protectively behind her. Stephanie and Sarah came next, bouncing energetically hand in hand. Maggie brought up the rear, her video camera in hand.

Elizabeth waited until Jessica got her campers set up. Jessica ran into the kitchen and emerged a moment later with a huge vat of potatoes and potato peelers, which she distributed to eager outstretched hands. Elizabeth shook her head. Leave it to Jessica to get her campers to help out with KP duty.

As soon as the group was busy working, Elizabeth hurried up to her sister. "Jessica, I need to talk to you!" she said urgently.

Jessica turned to face her. "Oh, hi, Liz," she calmly replied.

"Oh, hi, Liz," the campers echoed.

Jessica rolled her eyes. "And I thought it was bad enough having *one* twin!"

The campers rolled their eyes in an exaggerated imitation of Jessica, swooning in frustration.

"Liz, I don't think this is a good time," Jessica said, raking her fingers through her hair. Soon six hands followed suit. Jessica dropped her hand quickly. She didn't reprimand the girls for imitating her, but Elizabeth could see her sister clench her jaw in frustration.

Maggie trained her video camera on the twins. Ever since she got to camp, Maggie had been taping

34

everything she saw. Particularly Jessica. Usually Jessica loved this kind of attention, but now it looked as though she'd had just about enough.

"Jess, I need to talk to you in private," Elizabeth said in a low voice.

"Can't it wait?" Jessica mouthed.

Elizabeth shook her head firmly and pulled her to the next table. The campers dropped their potato peelers and immediately surrounded them. "Jess, can't you do anything about them?" she complained.

"Elizabeth Wakefield! What do you think you're doing?" a scolding voice called across the mess hall.

Elizabeth wheeled around. It was Lacey, looking like an army sergeant. She was dressed all in green khaki and her hands were planted firmly on her ample hips.

"It's bad enough that you can't manage to do your own duties, but do you have to disrupt your sister while she executes hers beautifully?" Lacey lectured.

Elizabeth blanched. Lacey had an uncanny ability to show up at the wrong time—always when Elizabeth had stepped even the slightest bit out of line. And she didn't even seem to notice that Jessica wasn't actually performing her duties at all.

Lacey shook her head in disgust. "You two may look alike, but that's about all you've got in common," she said in her slow southern drawl.

Elizabeth's face burned. "U-uh . . . ," she stammered, searching for an excuse.

Jessica flashed Lacey a winning smile. "Please excuse my sister. She's not very responsible."

"Well, I'll let it go this time, but I don't want to

see you disturbing your sister again," Lacey said, waving her index finger at Elizabeth.

Elizabeth opened her mouth, but then shut it again. Shooting Jessica a dirty look, she turned and stormed away. She pushed through the swinging doors of the mess hall angrily and exited the lodge.

Elizabeth sighed as she walked out into the warm night air. Jessica was right. She wasn't very responsible anymore. In fact, she was acting more like Jessica than Jessica herself. Even though the twins were identical in appearance, from their long golden blond hair to their sparkling blue-green eyes to the matching dimple in their left cheek, they were completely different in character.

Elizabeth was usually the reliable twin. A straight-A student, she was a staff reporter for the school paper and was highly involved in extracurricular activities. While she liked to have a good time just as much as her sister did, Elizabeth always took care of her responsibilities first. And in her spare time, her favorite activities were quiet ones—writing in her journal, taking a walk with Todd, or going to a movie with her best friend, Enid Rollins.

Jessica, on the other hand, was usually the unreliable twin. Jessica had a good heart, but a daring soul. She had a tendency to get involved in scrapes and let Elizabeth get her out of them. For Jessica, schoolwork took a backseat to her three primary pursuits—cheerleading, parties, and shopping at the mall. And while Elizabeth had been with one boy forever, Jessica changed boyfriends almost as often as she changed shoes.

But now, it looked like their roles had reversed.

Elizabeth's normally boy-crazy sister had decided to have a boy-free summer, and Jessica's campers were so infatuated with her that they were trying to *become* her. Meanwhile steady, dependable Elizabeth Wakefield was cheating on her boyfriend and neglecting her counselor duties. Last week she had been so exhausted from sneaking out late at night to write the play that she couldn't keep her eyes open during the day. Rose Schwartz, the sailing counselor, had finally gotten so fed up with her that she told her she'd be more helpful in her cabin sleeping.

Elizabeth kicked at a tuft of dirt. Now that Todd had shown up, it didn't look like things were going to get better. Elizabeth's stomach tightened at the thought of the night ahead. She slumped down in a patch of grass and doodled with a stick in the dirt. Now she knew what it felt like to be Jessica. And she didn't like it.

Jessica dropped her potato peeler on the table and sat back, her mind whirring away. She was desperate to get Tanya alone to get the scoop on Paul. Something didn't seem right. If Paul really thought she was a dumb blonde with nothing between her ears, then why had he asked Tanya a million questions about her? And why did he give her a heart-stopping kiss?

Jessica was sure that Tanya would have some valuable information. But Jessica couldn't seem to shake the rest of her little charges for a minute. She twisted a lock of blond hair around her finger, deep in thought.

Suddenly all the potato peelers clattered onto the table. Startled, Jessica looked up. All the campers had stopped working and were twirling their hair between their fingers.

Jessica clapped quickly. "OK, back to work!" she instructed, picking up her potato peeler.

"Back to work!" Sofia intoned, her brown eyes large with admiration. She picked up her utensil and watched Jessica intently as she worked.

Jessica picked up a potato out of the sack and started peeling the skin off it. Suddenly she was hit with an idea.

"Who wants to play a game?" she asked the group.

"We do!" the girls yelled out simultaneously.

"OK, here are the rules," Jessica said. "We're going to play the Great Potato Peel. Whoever manages to finish all her potatoes first wins."

"What's the pwize?" Stephanie asked. Stephanie was an energetic little girl with frizzy red hair and freckles. She was missing her two front teeth and had a lisp.

"Whoever wins gets to be me for a day," Jessica replied.

"I wanna be Jessica!" Sarah yelled out. She was a pretty Chinese-American girl with straight black hair that fell to her shoulders. Grabbing a potato peeler from the table, she began whacking at a spud, sending bits of potato flying. Soon all the campers were peeling furiously.

"Not yet, not yet," Jessica said, holding up a hand. "You have to wait till I say 'Go!' Now, everybody has to work at different tables. I don't want any potato swapping."

Jessica assigned them each a sack of potatoes to peel. The girls grabbed their bags and flew to separate tables.

"Hey! This is my table!" Anastasia protested as Sarah joined her. Anastasia looked like a slightly older version of her sister, Sofia, except that she had blue eyes.

"I was here first!" Sarah responded.

Jessica hurried over to the commotion. She leaned down to Sarah and put an arm around her shoulders. "Look, why don't you take that big table on the boys' side? That's the best table."

"It is?" Sarah asked, looking up at her with an excited grin. Jessica nodded solemnly. Sarah picked up her bag and flew over to the other table.

"Everybody ready?" Jessica yelled out.

"Ready!" came a chorus of excited voices.

"On your mark, get set, GO!"

Jessica watched with a bemused smile as the girls worked intensely. There was total silence in the room. She knew Tanya would win. Most of the girls could barely get any skin off the potatoes at all. But Tanya spent most of every summer working in the kitchen at the diner. Her parents didn't have a lot of money and needed their kids to help out in the restaurant.

Sure enough, fifteen minutes later Tanya let forth a victorious cry. "First finished!"

The other campers jumped up, but Jessica held up a hand. "Everybody has to finish their pile."

Jessica went over to inspect Tanya's work.

"Wow, you did a great job!" Jessica enthused, taking a seat on the bench next to the girl.

Tanya gave her a big gap-toothed smile. "I always help out at the restaurant," she said somewhat shyly.

"I bet your brother appreciates all your help," Jessica said.

Tanya made a face. "He thinks I'm just in the way."

Jessica put an arm around the girl's shoulders. "Big brothers are always like that," she said reassuringly.

"Do you have a big brother?" Tanya asked.

Jessica nodded. "His name is Steven. He always has lots of girlfriends."

"Bleah!" Tanya exclaimed, picking up a big potato and standing it on its end. "Hello, Mr. Potato," she said, and giggled. Then she pulled her barrettes out of her hair and stuck them in the sides like arms.

"Your brother must have lots of girlfriends, too," Jessica said.

Tanya shook her head silently, studying the potato intensely. She reached into her bag and pulled out her arts-and-crafts supplies. She turned the little plastic bag of supplies upside down. Buttons and beads spilled out on the table.

Jessica bent down to retrieve a button that had fallen on the floor. "Why doesn't he have any girlfriends?" she asked casually, sticking two buttons in the potato like eyes.

Tanya clapped in glee and winked at the potato. "Because he's stupid," she said.

"There must be a better reason than that," Jessica said.

"Well, ac-tually, some counselor was mean to him and now he hates girls," Tanya said, turning her head sideways to inspect her creation. She stuck a needle in the middle of the head and started giggling. "Look!" she said, covering her mouth with her hand as she snickered. "Needle nose!" Then she added a series of beads to the bottom of the head, forming a big, crooked smile.

"A girl hurt him?" Jessica asked. "What girl?"

Tanya shrugged. "I don't know. Some JC last summer."

*So that explains Paul's nasty note,* Jessica thought. Her gut instinct had told her there was more to Paul's note than his lack of interest in her. But Jessica wasn't going to let it go yet. She planned to get to the bottom of the story.

Jessica drummed her fingers on the table. She knew just where to go to get the information she needed. To Suzanne, the arts counselor. She'd been at Camp Echo Mountain for years. And she knew all.

Elizabeth squared her jaw and marched through the door of the lodge for dinner, feeling as if she was about to face her doom. She had no idea what Nicole had cooked up, but she had a feeling it wasn't going to be pretty. Elizabeth had considered skipping dinner altogether but had decided that could be even more dangerous. With Nicole, Todd, and Joey alone, anything could happen.

As she walked into the crowded mess hall she

41

scanned the room quickly. The cafeteria was a large room with a dozen rows of tables. The girls' tables were on one side of the aisle and the boys' were on the other.

Elizabeth breathed a sigh of relief as she realized that Todd wasn't there yet. Then her blue-green eyes locked with Joey's deep green ones. Elizabeth tried to read his expression, but he just stared at her coldly. He picked up his tray and walked pointedly to the opposite side of his table, sitting with his back toward her.

Elizabeth winced and headed to the dinner line. Lacey had given Todd strict orders that he could only see Elizabeth in the evenings. She didn't want Todd to distract Elizabeth at her sailing post or during meals. Lacey had insinuated that Elizabeth was having problems with her duties. "Adjustment problems," she had told Todd on the phone. For once, Elizabeth was grateful to Lacey. If she could just avoid Todd during meals, maybe Joey wouldn't have to see them together.

Elizabeth gritted her teeth as she picked up a tray and joined the line of chattering campers. She didn't think she could bear facing her obnoxious group of ten-year-old girls. Her campers had shown her no respect since day one. Ever since Aimee had dubbed her "Dizzy Lizzie," the name had caught on with the whole camp. Now most people just called her "Diz."

Yesterday she'd thought her relationship with her charges was improving. Jessica had called all the campers to the main lodge for a special presentation. She had revealed the incriminating video proving

42

Nicole had stolen Elizabeth's play, and Elizabeth's campers had rallied around her. Elizabeth had been gratified by her campers' support, but it turned out the change was short lived. This morning at breakfast they'd been back to their usual bratty selves.

*Well, I've had enough of it,* Elizabeth decided as she took a plate of macaroni and cheese. She was sick and tired of accepting her campers' abuse. She was going to make them respect her if it was the last thing she did. Feeling determined, she grabbed her tray and headed for her table.

"Liz, sit here!" Aimee called as she reached the table, shifting over to give her room on the bench.

"What did you call me?" Elizabeth asked aggressively. Then she stopped as she registered the words.

"Is it okay if we call you Liz?" Aimee asked.

"Or do you prefer Elizabeth?" Helen asked, pushing her huge tortoiseshell glasses up on her nose.

Elizabeth narrowed her eyes, feeling somewhat suspicious. She was sure Aimee had something up her sleeve. Aimee was the leader of the pack, and Helen tended to be her echo. "Liz is fine," Elizabeth said cautiously.

"We just loved your play," Emily gushed. Emily was a tall girl with honey blond hair and soft brown eyes.

"All of us went to play tryouts today," Adrienne added, her light green eyes flashing with excitement.

"I got the part of the cook," Jennifer put in.

*That's appropriate,* Elizabeth thought. A stocky girl with auburn hair and hazel eyes, Jennifer loved to eat. If she wasn't shoving food in her mouth, she was playing with it or dropping it on her clothes.

"And Ashley and I are senior counselors," Emily said.

Elizabeth had trouble distinguishing between Ashley and Emily. They were inseparable, and they resembled each other. They were both tall and willowy, with blond hair and cultivated demeanors. But while Emily's hair was honey blond, Ashley's was platinum.

Elizabeth smiled at the girls. It was the first genuine smile she'd given them all summer. "That's terrific, you guys," she said.

"Are you a writer?" Helen asked, her satin dark eyes round with awe.

"Well, I'd like to be," Elizabeth said.

"Do you think the camp legend's true?" Jennifer asked, pushing her food around on her plate.

"I don't know, but just the other day an eerie thing happened to me," Elizabeth said. She leaned toward the girls, her expression serious. "It was late at night and I was returning from the dock. It was pitch-dark out and a full moon was shining in the dense woods. There was total silence. All that could be heard was the crunching of my shoes. Crunch, crunch, crunch."

The girls were huddled close together, listening in silent anticipation.

"When suddenly—" Elizabeth paused to let the tension build up, then she dropped her voice to a whisper. "I heard the sounds of chopping wood."

Jennifer jumped and Helen screamed. Then they all laughed.

"I got chills down my spine," Ashley declared, twirling a lock of wavy blond hair.

"Is that true?" Emily demanded.

Elizabeth nodded, her blue-green eyes twinkling. "Cross my heart."

Suddenly Elizabeth felt a kiss on her cheek. She looked up to find Todd standing behind her, a bouquet of wildflowers in his hand. "Oh, thanks, Todd," Elizabeth said, trying to look pleased as she took the bouquet.

Helen let out a long whistle.

"Liz's got a boyfriend! Liz's got a boyfriend!" Jennifer chanted in an obnoxious voice.

Elizabeth's face flamed as the rest of the girls picked up the chant. "Girls, calm down!" she said sharply. She was sure the sound could carry across the aisle to Joey's table.

"Todd, you better go sit with Winston," Elizabeth said, her expression serious. "You're creating a commotion."

"OK, Liz, sorry," Todd said, looking concerned. "I'll catch you later."

But at that moment Nicole appeared. "Well, just the couple I was looking for," she said, sidling up to them with a sweet smile. "I've got a little surprise for you."

"I'm sure you do," Elizabeth responded, her face grim.

"I've set up a romantic table for two in the corner," Nicole said, her smile becoming a smirk. Elizabeth glanced over and saw an elegant table standing smack in the middle of the room. A red-checkered cloth was draped over it and little white candles were laid out in the center. The table was in plain view of the entire camp.

Elizabeth tried to return Nicole's fake grin. "Nicole, that was really nice of you, but Lacey wouldn't allow it."

Nicole waved a dismissive hand. "Don't worry. She's at the theater in town tonight."

"Nicole, you know I can't leave my campers alone," Elizabeth protested.

"Lacey took my group on a field trip to see a play, so I can watch your campers for you," Nicole replied.

"I'm sure they wouldn't be happy about that," Elizabeth said in a low voice, though she knew they'd be thrilled. Her campers loved Nicole. Nicole was the waterskiing JC, and all the campers thought she was cool because she could do flips on her skis.

Unfortunately Adrienne picked up the conversation. "That's okay, Elizabeth. We don't mind if Nicole sits with us."

Nicole gave Elizabeth a bright smile. "See? I thought of everything!"

*You sure did,* Elizabeth thought bitterly. She stood up reluctantly and went over to the table in the middle of the room.

"Isn't this romantic?" Todd asked as he took a seat at the table. He picked up a bunch of matches and lit the tiny white candles in the center of the tablecloth.

Elizabeth nodded as she sat down opposite him. She had never felt so exposed in her whole life. As Todd poured her a cup of bug juice from the glass pitcher on the table, Elizabeth stole a look at Joey.

His jaw was set in a determined line and he stared over her head.

"To us!" Todd toasted, picking up his plastic cup of bug juice.

"To us," Elizabeth repeated tonelessly.

"And one more thing," Todd added, holding his cup in the air. "To Nicole!"

Elizabeth couldn't respond. She jabbed her fork into her macaroni and cheese and brought a forkful to her mouth. She didn't know when she'd been so miserable.

# Chapter 3

"And now, the famous Santini brothers will demonstrate the proper form for a tumble!" Winston announced on Tuesday morning at the gymnastics cabin. "Boys, please hold your applause until the demonstration is over."

Winston and Todd were leading the morning tumbling workshop for a group of twelve-year-old boys. Derek was helping Jessica out at the dance cabin for the day, so Winston and Todd were alone. As Winston didn't know the first thing about tumbling, he was glad Todd was there to help him out.

The boys laughed as Winston assumed position for a somersault. "Legs bent, chest out, arms out." He gave the boys a stern look. "And remember, appearance is everything. Execution is nothing." Winston tried to keep a straight face as he pumped out his narrow chest. He knew he looked ridiculous. He was wearing bright pink polka-dotted biking shorts and a canary yellow sleeveless T-shirt.

Winston put his arms out in front of him as if he were about to dive into water and sprang forward. He leapt awkwardly into the air and fell into a clumsy somersault, gangly arms and legs flying. Todd followed right behind with a line of smooth somersaults.

Winston stood up and wiped off his knees to the sound of spontaneous applause. He gave the boys a goofy grin. "Thank you, thank you."

"OK, guys, line up," Todd instructed. "It's your turn."

"And remember, form, posture, grace!" Winston added.

The boys all ran forward and did a line of somersaults.

"And now we're going to take it in the air," Winston said as the boys stood up. He jumped up on a mini-trampoline and started bouncing. All the boys hopped up on trampolines and followed him.

"Keep your knees bent and your center of gravity low," he instructed. "Now, watch closely as I demonstrate an aerial flip," Winston said. He bounced higher and higher, gaining momentum with each jump. Suddenly he sprang into the air. "Whoa!" he yelled as he lost control and flew across the room. He instinctively curled his body as he landed on the mat, somersaulting wildly across the floor.

Winston stood up and grinned at the boys. "That's what I call the famous 'somersault jump.' But that's a little advanced for you at this point.

Please stay on your trampolines at all times."

Winston wiped his brow, a little worn out from his demonstration. He looked at his watch. Half the session had already gone by. "Hey, Todd, you want to take over?" he asked. Todd was going to give the boys an introduction to basic karate.

"Sure, Winston," Todd agreed. "Everybody grab a mat. Now the first thing we're going to learn is a scissors kick."

Winston slid down the wall and sat on a mat in the corner. Digging through his backpack, he pulled out a crumpled letter that he'd been carrying around with him all day. It was from his girlfriend, Maria Santelli. Winston really missed her. They'd been separated for almost two weeks now, but it felt like two years. Maria was spending the summer at her grandmother's ranch.

Winston looked at the letter in anticipation. He'd just gotten it this morning, but he hadn't had a moment to himself to read it. He looked up to make sure none of the boys were near. But they were all busy imitating the karate move that Todd was demonstrating.

Winston ripped open the letter and skimmed the contents eagerly.

> *Dear Winston,*
>    *Life on the ranch is better than ever. . . .*
> *Went horseback riding today with Hank, the*
> *cowboy. . . . Later Hank showed me how to*
> *milk cows. . . . Hank can lasso a bull's horns*
> *from a hundred feet away. . . .*

Winston frowned, realizing that Maria had mentioned the same guy in the last three letters—it was getting to him.

Winston pictured Maria and Hank riding bareback on a white stallion. Maria was wearing jeans and a denim shirt tied at the midriff. Her frizzy brown hair was wrapped up in a bandanna, and her pretty hazel eyes were sparkling with pleasure. Hank, the all-American macho stud of a cowboy, had brown hair and light blue eyes. The two of them galloped across the plains. All Maria could feel was the wind whipping through her hair and Hank's strong, golden arms wrapped around her bare waist.

Winston looked at his pale, gangly arms in disgust. He wouldn't even be able to climb up on a horse. *How can I compete with a cowboy?* he asked himself sadly.

Winston fell onto his back and stared unseeingly at the ceiling. He knew the answer to his own question. *I can't.*


"Can you believe the nerve of that girl?" Elizabeth vented to Maria in the kitchen before lunch. "Last night Nicole made a cozy little dinner for me and Todd and set out the table right in front of the entire camp."

"And right in front of Joey," Maria said wryly.

"Exactly," Elizabeth said, picking up a turnip and dicing it. She was still steaming from Nicole's prank the night before.

Elizabeth and Maria had been assigned KP duty for lunch, and they were in the kitchen chopping vegetables. The camp kitchen was a vast room, with endless counter space and huge steel sinks. An array of copper pots in all sizes hung from the walls, and a big brass kettle was nestled in an old-fashioned red brick fireplace in the corner.

Elizabeth shifted her stool closer to the counter and examined the selection of fresh summer vegetables set out before her. There were bright green and yellow peppers, oversize cucumbers, plump red tomatoes, and bags of turnips and onions. She picked out a yellow pepper and laid it on the cutting board in front of her.

Maria chopped up a cucumber neatly and threw the slices in a huge ceramic bowl. "That wasn't a very nice move on Nicole's part," she said, smiling at Elizabeth sympathetically.

"Not nice!" Elizabeth protested. "It was evil." She picked up the pepper and whacked through it with a cutting knife, splitting it apart in one clean gesture.

"Whoa!" Maria said. "That's a yellow pepper you're chopping there, not Nicole's head."

"I wish it *were* Nicole's head," Elizabeth muttered, setting the pepper down on the cutting board and slicing it in long, thin strips.

Maria set down her knife and looked at Elizabeth carefully. "Maybe you're blaming the wrong person for this situation. It takes two to tango."

Elizabeth's face flushed as Maria's words struck home. "You're right, Maria," she admitted. "*I'm* the one who's gotten myself into this situation. *I'm* the one who was cheating on Todd. And lying to Joey about it. It serves me right to have Todd show up."

"Well, I don't know about that, but it seems to me that the only way out now is to come clean," Maria said. She grabbed a slice of pepper from the cutting board and crunched into it.

Elizabeth looked at Maria in dismay. "You mean tell Todd I've been seeing Joey?"

Maria nodded. "And tell Joey the truth about Todd. Maybe he would understand the situation. Or maybe he wouldn't mind just dating for the summer."

"There's no way Joey would accept that," Elizabeth said. "And Todd would never forgive me."

"But you wouldn't be torn apart by guilt anymore," Maria pointed out. "And I wouldn't have to listen to you complain about it anymore."

Elizabeth dropped her head in her hands. "Ugh," she moaned. "What a mess."

Maria gave Elizabeth a smile. "Or maybe there's another way out," she added. "What were you planning to do?"

Elizabeth shrugged and looked abashed. "I thought I'd just wait it out and avoid Joey for a few days."

Maria shook her head disapprovingly. "Elizabeth Wakefield, you have got to make a choice."

Elizabeth looked at her in despair. "But how?"

"Simple," Maria said, peeling the outside skin of an onion. "Just trust your feelings." She chopped up the onion and tears came to her eyes. Grabbing a towel from the counter, she ran it under water and dabbed at her eyes. "Are you happy to see Todd?"

Elizabeth shook her head. "No, I'm miserable."

"Well, then, it's clear," Maria said in a matter-of-fact tone.

"I guess it is," Elizabeth conceded, nodding slowly. Maria was right. She had to tell Todd the truth. Even though she and Todd had a long and wonderful history together, she had to face the facts. She was attracted to somebody else. She had to break up with Todd.

Just the thought made her feel like the most disloyal girlfriend on earth.

"I guess we've got to play some *stupid* game to entertain the little kiddies." Winston scowled as he surveyed the field later that afternoon. Winston and Aaron's ten-year-old campers had gathered in the field outside the main lodge to play sports together before dinner.

Todd looked at Winston in surprise. Winston loved kids. In fact, it had been Winston's idea to get the boys together. He had been all fired up about the idea that morning. "A great sports-off!" he had announced at the mess hall after breakfast.

Actually, Todd surmised, Winston had been in a foul mood ever since his tumbling accident that morning. It was as if he'd had a personality transformation in the last few hours. Todd wondered if he'd gotten hurt from his fall. Or maybe he had been embarrassed. But that wasn't like Winston. At Sweet Valley High, Winston had a reputation as the class clown, and there was nothing he liked better than making people laugh.

"OK, what's the game of the hour?" Aaron asked, marching up to them. A gang of boys followed quickly behind.

"Throw the boys in the lake," Winston muttered under his breath.

Aaron looked at Todd questioningly. Todd lifted his eyebrows and shrugged.

Johnny, one of Aaron's campers, raced up to them. "Let's play Cowboys and Indians!" he yelled.

"We're the cowboys!" one of Winston's campers claimed. He was a towheaded boy named Bryan, and he was the smallest camper of the group.

"And we're the Indians!" Jacob of Aaron's group screamed. He scrambled a few yards away and took a position behind a grassy knoll. When he reached the base of the hill, he picked up a stick and drew an imaginary line in the grass. "This here is Indian territory," he announced.

Winston marched up the little hill and stared down at the boys. He looked like he was about to explode. "Just what do you think you're doing?" he asked.

"We're preparing for battle," Bryan declared. He dived onto the grass on his stomach on the other side of the knoll and held an imaginary gun out in front of him. Tad, a pudgy boy with a crewcut, jumped down next to him.

"Oh, that's a great idea," Winston said, snorting sarcastically. "Have any of you given a moment's thought to the meaning of 'Cowboys and Indians'?"

Todd gave Aaron a worried look. Had Winston gone over the edge?

Little Bryan looked at him wide eyed and shook his head.

"Well, I'll tell you the meaning," Winston went on. "The Indians were living peaceably off the land when the American settlers came over from Europe and invaded the country. They slaughtered all the Native Americans and took over their territory." Winston stared the boys down. "And now all you kids just think it's a fun game."

"It *is* a fun game!" Tad screamed out.

"Whoop, whoop, whoop, whoop!" little Jacob yelled, clapping a hand over his mouth and doing an Indian war dance.

"What's the point?" Winston yelled. "The cowboys win every time anyway!"

The boys looked at him like he was nuts, then Jacob picked up an imaginary arrow and shot at a little boy. "Ping!" he yelled.

"Bang bang bang!" a cowboy shouted.

"Get back, Apaches!" another boy shouted.

Soon a full-fledged war had ensued and Winston stomped away.

"What's eating him?" Aaron asked.

"I don't know, but we better find out," Todd said.

Todd and Aaron followed Winston. He was sitting under a tree, glowering.

Aaron crouched down on the ground next to him. "Hey, man, don't worry, maybe the Indians will win this time," he said placatingly.

"I wish they'd killed all the cowboys in the first place," Winston said bitterly.

Todd looked at his friend oddly. Maybe the heat was getting to him. "I didn't realize you had such a thing about cowboys," he said carefully.

Winston sighed. "Well, just one, actually," he admitted.

"OK, give," Todd said, sliding down on the grass next to him.

Winston looked around to make sure they weren't being overheard by any other campers. "Well, you know Maria's staying with her grandmother on a ranch this summer, right?"

Todd and Aaron nodded.

"I've gotten a number of letters from her, and she always mentions the same guy," Winston explained. "His name is Hank, and he's a cowboy."

"And you think she's fallen for him," Todd said.

Winston nodded.

Aaron looked skeptical. "A cowboy? Maria?"

"Read this," Winston said, handing him the letter. Aaron unfolded the page, frowning as he skimmed the contents. Todd read over his shoulder.

"It doesn't sound good," Todd had to concede.

"See? I told you," Winston said. He dropped his head in his hands. "It's so humiliating. Left for a cowboy." Winston sighed. "I'll never live this down at school. I can just hear the jokes. 'Winston was away at camp for the summer. Meanwhile, back at the ranch . . .'"

Aaron laughed, and Winston gave him a dirty look.

Todd thought for a minute. Winston and Maria had been going out forever. They always seemed perfectly suited to each other. "So what are you going to do about it?" he asked.

Winston shrugged sadly. "What can I do about it? If she wants another guy, then she can have him."

Todd looked straight at him, a challenge in his

eyes. "You mean you're just going to give up that easily?"

"Doesn't Maria mean anything to you?" Aaron added.

"Do you two have a better idea?" Winston returned.

Todd nodded and looked at Aaron, a glint in his eye. "As a matter of fact, I think I do."

Winston looked from one boy to the other, an expression of alarm on his face. "Uh-oh, I know that look. That look means trouble."

Todd smiled. "Winston, baby, we're going to turn you into a cowboy," he said.

"Oh, no, you're not," Winston responded.

"It'll be simple," Aaron reassured him. "A pair of cowboy boots, a cowboy hat, and you'll be set."

Winston raised his hands in protest. "The answer is no, and that's final. I don't want to hear another word about cowboys. I'm taking off. See you guys later." Winston turned and stalked away.

Aaron winked at Todd after Winston left. "He'll come around," he said confidently.

Wanting to sulk for a while, Winston decided to take out a canoe. He needed to be alone.

Winston headed into the boathouse. A row of aluminum canoes were lined up against the far wall. Grabbing the rope of the nearest canoe, he dragged it through the door. As he pulled it onto the sand he stumbled and stubbed his toe, whacking himself in the back of the knees with the boat. "Ouch," he muttered, scowling to himself.

It was no wonder Maria didn't want to be with him anymore, Winston thought as he tugged on the string. With his knobby knees and gangly arms, Winston knew he was a joke of a boyfriend. He'd always thought that Maria loved him for his clumsiness. She'd always said it was endearing that he had two left feet. But now he knew the truth. She had loved him *despite* his clumsiness. And now she didn't love him at all.

Winston sighed as he pushed the canoe into the murky green lake. He felt like he'd lost half of himself. He and Maria had been together forever, and they were always the center of the crowd.

Everybody liked Maria. She was pretty and funny and involved in everything—the student council, her sorority, cheerleading. Maria was perfect for him. But obviously he wasn't perfect for her. She didn't want some knobby-kneed clown. She wanted a real man. A cowboy.

Winston reached into the boat and pulled out an orange life vest. Slipping his arms into it, he threw off his shoes and climbed into the canoe. Then he grabbed an oar and shoved off into the water.

"Mind if I join you?" called a husky voice from the shore. Winston looked back. A redheaded girl was standing at the water's edge, holding her shoes in her hand. He'd thought he met all the counselors, but he'd never seen her before.

*Yes, I do mind,* Winston thought. But he just shrugged. He didn't see that he had much choice. Saying no would just be rude.

The girl dropped her shoes in the sand and

59

jumped into the canoe, taking a seat on the bench at the back end. "You're Winston, aren't you?" she asked as she wriggled into a life vest.

Winston nodded and paddled silently.

"I'm Lara O'Mally," the girl said. "I'm in Nicole's group." She picked up an oar and paddled in unison with him.

"You're a camper?" Winston asked.

"Yeah, I'm just fifteen," Lara said.

Winston looked at the girl in surprise. She might be fifteen, but she looked like she was eighteen. She was average height, with wild curly red hair, smooth white skin, and a smattering of freckles. "You look like you could be a counselor," Winston said.

"I just missed the JC cutoff," Lara explained. They hit a bend in the lake, and Lara expertly paddled backward, sending them in a smooth turn. "In fact, I'm going to turn sixteen on the last day of camp. I tried to get Lacey to make an exception for me, but she refused. You know how Lacey is."

"I'm not surprised," Winston said. "Old iron-will Cavannah won't make an exception for anything."

Lara laughed a golden laugh that seemed to bounce across the sun-dappled water. "I thought she was going to explode the other night when you imitated her in the auditorium."

Winston laughed as well, feeling his spirits pick up. The campers had practically fallen asleep while watching an adventure film, so he thought he should liven up the atmosphere with a few antics. The kids had gone wild when he launched into a Lacey impersonation.

Unfortunately Lacey had caught him right in the middle of it. Ever since then, he hadn't exactly been in the camp owner's favor. In fact, she had threatened to kick him out. "Undermining my authority undermines your authority as well," she had lectured him. "One more stunt like that from you and you're out."

"My timing wasn't very good." Winston grinned.

"Actually, your timing was perfect," Lara said. "I thought I was going to break a rib, I was laughing so hard."

Suddenly a loud motorboat whizzed by, sending a ripple of waves in its wake. A water-skier was holding on to a rope attached to the back of the boat.

"Oh, sorry!" the water-skier yelled.

The canoe lurched dangerously in the rough water. "Uh-oh." Winston gulped as the massive waves threatened to make the boat capsize.

"Lean to the left," Lara instructed. "Put all your weight into the direction of the wave and hold your oar firm in the water." Within moments they had maneuvered the canoe out of the current.

"Wow, you're pretty good at this," Winston told Lara as they reached still waters.

"My family has a cottage on Lake Ontario," Lara explained. "I've spent a lot of summers out on the water."

They paddled out to the middle of the lake and let the boat drift. "Ah, this is the life," Winston said, leaning back against an extra life vest and closing his eyes. He felt himself relax for the first time all day.

"So, do you have a girlfriend?" Lara asked.

Winston hesitated. Even though he had just met

Lara, he found himself wanting to confide in her. He'd felt comfortable with her from the first moment she sat down in the canoe, and Winston instinctively trusted her. And it would be helpful to get a female perspective.

"Well, I used to," Winston said. Then he opened up to her, telling her about his concerns regarding Maria.

Lara looked stunned. "I can't believe a girl would cheat on you!" she exclaimed. "If you were my boyfriend, I'd treat you right," she added.

Winston flushed with pleasure. It was nice to be appreciated—even if he could never act on it. JCs dating campers was *strictly* forbidden.

Winston gave her a sidelong glance. "What kind of cowboy do you think I'd make?" he asked.

"A very sexy one," Lara answered in a husky voice.

# Chapter 4

"Jessica! Where are you running off to?" Lila demanded on Tuesday night after dinner. Bo was standing next to her. Even though Lila drove her crazy
talking about Bo, Jessica had to admit that they made
a nice couple. Bo was wearing beige cotton shorts
and a blue polo shirt, and Lila had on a pale yellow
cotton dress. They both looked tanned and healthy.
And happy.

"A bunch of JCs are going to make a campfire and
cook s'mores," Bo said. "You should join us."

Jessica searched for a quick excuse. "Uh, I was
just going back to the cabin to change."

Lila looked at her suspiciously. "Change for
*what*?" she asked.

"For the game of Sardines later on tonight,"
Jessica said. "It's getting a little chilly."

"Sardines?" Lila and Bo exclaimed in unison.

"Don't you eat them?" Bo asked.

"Oh, gross," Lila said, crinkling her nose in disgust. "We're going to eat sardines tonight?"

Jessica had to laugh. "You two were definitely not made for camp. Sardines is just the name of the game. One person, the sardine, hides, and everyone else splits up and goes to look for him or her. If you find the sardine, you join in the hiding place. And so on, until only one person is left. That person loses and has to be the next sardine."

"Hmm, that doesn't sound so bad," Lila said with a grin. She leaned back in Bo's arms.

"I'll hide with you anytime, baby," Bo said, tightening his arms around her waist.

"Do you guys mind if I leave before I retch?" Jessica asked.

They laughed. "All right, we'll see you later," Lila said.

Jessica waved and walked off casually, trying to look natural. But as soon as she rounded the corner of the lodge, she picked up the pace. She walked briskly up the dirt path that led through the woods to the girls' cabins. She wanted to see Suzanne, the arts counselor. She had tried to get hold of her at the arts cabin earlier in the day, but Suzanne had been up to her elbows in papier-mâché. Suzanne had invited Jessica to stop by after dinner, and Jessica wanted to see her before the rest of the senior counselors returned to the cabin.

A few minutes later Jessica exited the woods and made her way to the female senior counselors' cabin. A little out of breath, she knocked sharply on the wooden door.

"C'mon in!" came a cheery voice. Jessica pushed open the door and peeked her head inside. Suzanne was propped up against the wall, a pair of purple jeans in her lap and knitting needles in her hand. She was a pretty girl with a halo of wild, frizzy brown hair and a funky style of dressing.

"Hi, Jess!" she said, dropping her needles on the bed and waving her inside.

"Wow, this is nice," Jessica said, taking in the senior counselors' cabin. The cabin was big and airy, with a high peaked ceiling and a woven Mexican rug on the floor. The women had decorated the walls with avant-garde posters and personal artwork. A Chinese lantern glittered on a small wooden table.

"Seniority has its privileges," Suzanne said. "Here, have a seat." She cleared off a space and patted a place on the bunk next to her.

Jessica sat down and fingered the jeans on the bed. A yellow butterfly was embroidered on one knee and a long red flower traveled down the length of the other leg. "Hey, these are cool," Jessica said.

"You like them?" Suzanne asked, holding up the jeans for inspection. They tapered in at the knees and flared out wildly at the bottom. "It's sort of a seventies retro look. I thought I could wear them with platform shoes."

"Do you always make your own clothes?" Jessica asked.

"I usually just embellish them a little," Suzanne said. "I spend a lot of time poking around thrift shops." She threw the jeans across the bed. "But I don't think you stopped by to talk about my fashion interests."

"Yeah, actually, I have a slight dilemma that I thought you might be able to help me with," Jessica explained.

"What's the dilemma?" Suzanne asked. Then she held up a hand. "Wait, let me guess. What kind of problem would Jessica Wakefield have?" She snapped her fingers. "I've got it! Love problems!"

Jessica laughed. "You hit the nail on the head." She leaned in closer to Suzanne. "Listen, you've got to be totally confidential about this."

"Nothing leaves this cabin," Suzanne reassured her.

"Well, I met this guy," Jessica began. "He's the brother of one of my campers—"

"And his name is Paul Mathis," Suzanne finished.

Jessica looked at her in astonishment. "How did you know that?"

"Paul was a hot item here last summer. He was dating a blond junior counselor named Celia. It was pretty hot and heavy. But Celia was actually just using him to make her boyfriend jealous. Paul was crushed when he found out. And humiliated. He vowed never to have anything to do with the camp—or its counselors—again." Suzanne shook her head. "That boy's quite a character. I can still see him peeling out of here in his red pickup truck."

"I thought it was something like that," Jessica said. "That explains why Paul's been treating me so badly." She pondered the information for a moment. "The question is, what to do now?"

"In my opinion, I would stay as far away from Paul Mathis and his pickup truck as possible," Suzanne said.

66

"You would?" Jessica asked in dismay.

Suzanne nodded. "That boy's an impossible nut to crack. I don't think any girl can get through to him at this point. You'd be wasting your time."

Jessica smiled. "Well, I think Paul Mathis has met his match."

Suzanne cocked her head and sized up Jessica. "Maybe you're right. But it's not going to be easy to break through to him," she warned. "If you want to go out with Paul, you're going to have to fight for it."

Jessica nodded. That's exactly what she was planning to do.


"Aha! Perfect!" Todd exclaimed, digging out a red flannel shirt from his duffel bag. "This shirt has got cowboy written all over it."

Winston eyed the shirt in alarm and sank down on the bunk. Todd, Winston, and Aaron were in the boys' cabin after dinner, and Todd and Aaron were intent on enacting their plan. They were going to transform Winston into a cowboy—whether he wanted it or not.

"Pay dirt!" Aaron yelled from the opposite side of the cabin, where he was rummaging through his trunk. He held up a brown leather studded belt in one hand and a blue bandanna in the other.

Winston groaned and put his head in his hands. For the hundredth time that evening, he wanted to kick himself. Why did he ever confide in Todd and Aaron?

"Guys," Winston protested weakly. "Do you really think this is a good idea?"

Aaron looked stunned. "A good idea?"

"It's a great idea," Todd asserted.

"A brilliant idea," Aaron added.

"But what's the point of dressing up like a cowboy when Maria isn't even here to see me?" Winston asked.

"The point is to *practice*," Todd responded.

"You can't just become a cowboy overnight," Aaron elaborated. "You've got to feel the part. You've got to *live* the part. If Maria saw you today, she'd never believe you. But in a few weeks she's going to be looking at an authentic macho cowpoke."

Winston scowled. "This is an entire waste of time. It's too late now, anyway. Maria's already got her cowboy."

"But not for long," Todd said. "The summer is short, but the school year is long. You are going to return to Sweet Valley a changed man."

"A ruined man is more like it," Winston said.

"OK, enough of your whining," Todd said, urging Winston up. Winston reluctantly put on the shirt, tucking the ends into his jeans. Aaron threw him the belt and wrapped the bandanna around his neck cowboy style.

After he'd fastened the belt, Winston stepped back and looked at his reflection in the window, feeling relieved. He looked perfectly normal. Lots of guys wore plaid flannel shirts. "OK, great, guys, thanks," Winston said, jumping up to leave the cabin. "Let's go play Sardines with the rest of the group."

"Not so fast," Todd said, grabbing his arm.

"This is just the beginning," Aaron added.

Winston sat back down on the bunk reluctantly.

"Winston, man, look what we've got for you," Todd said. He fished around in a bag and pulled out a big straw cowboy hat. Aaron held up a worn pair of brown leather cowboy boots.

"Oh, boy," Winston said under his breath. "Where did you get those?"

"From the drama cabin," Todd said proudly.

"We just 'borrowed' a few things," Aaron added.

Todd stood the boots on the floor and Winston stepped into them. Then Aaron plopped the straw hat on his head, pulling the brim down low on his forehead. Winston stood up, feeling absolutely ridiculous.

Todd stepped back to inspect. "Good-bye, knobby-kneed Winston Egbert!" he said.

"Hello, Cowboy!" Aaron said.

Winston took a few tentative steps. The bandanna was choking his neck, the cowboy hat was blocking his vision, and the boots were too large. "I can barely walk in these things," he said. "They're a couple of sizes too big."

"That doesn't matter," Aaron said, waving a dismissive hand. "You look the part, and that's what counts."

"Looking like a cowboy isn't going to make me a cowboy," Winston complained.

"Don't worry," Aaron reassured him. "This is just the first step."

Winston moaned. That's what he was afraid of.

"With a few weeks practice you'll have all the skills of a cowboy down pat," Todd said.

"I'll make sure of it," Aaron reassured him. "If Maria likes cowboys, she won't be able to resist you."

Later that evening Elizabeth wandered around in the dark with her penlight, taking part in the JC game of Sardines. She had gotten to the main picnic area late, hoping to avoid Todd. The game was already in motion. Joey was the first sardine, and everybody was searching for him.

That is, everybody but Elizabeth. Joey was the last person she wanted to find. Joey hated her by now. Their conversation on the dock Sunday night came back to her. Joey had been completely honest with her. He had been attracted to Elizabeth from the start, but then he had been taken in by Nicole's pack of lies. Elizabeth was the one he really wanted. "But what about you and Todd?" he had asked.

"Oh, we're free to date other people," Elizabeth had answered lightly. She had heard herself lying but couldn't seem to stop herself. Then the next thing she knew, Joey's lips were on hers. Elizabeth kicked at a piece of wood in her way. Why hadn't she told him the truth? Now she was flaunting her relationship with Todd in front of him. Elizabeth sighed. *Have I messed everything up with Joey for good?* she wondered.

The sounds of boys' voices carried through the forest and Elizabeth stood perfectly still. She wasn't in the mood to socialize, and she wanted to keep out of Todd's sight.

"Man, I can barely walk in these things," Winston complained.

"Sure you can," came Aaron's voice.

Elizabeth ducked behind a tree. She was sure Todd was with Aaron and Winston. She held her breath as the boys walked loudly by her.

"Just put one foot in front of the other," Todd called out as they passed.

When she was sure they were gone, Elizabeth stepped out of her hiding place. Shining her penlight in front of her, she walked deeper into the brush.

Elizabeth crunched on some leaves and jumped, feeling spooked. It was scary walking around in the woods alone. The moon illuminated the forest in an eerie way, casting crisscrossing shadows of branches on the floor. Elizabeth felt like she was in a haunted forest. Rocks winked at her from the narrow path in front of her, and the tree trunks swayed ominously in the wind.

As she ducked under a tree with low branches a pair of gnarly arms reached out and snagged her hair. Elizabeth screamed and sucked in her breath. Yanking her hair out of the branch, she ran down the path and made her way out onto the main field where the rest of the JCs were.

Elizabeth breathed a sigh of relief as she exited the forest. Then she slowed, trying to bring down her pulse. Sounds of giggling wafted to her from the picnic area. Everybody was having a good time except her. Elizabeth was miserable. This was the stupidest game she had ever played.

As she stood in the middle of the field she hesitated. She couldn't stay out here in the open or she would bump into Todd. Sighing, she entered the forest on the opposite side.

71

Suddenly a hissing sound came from the shadows. Elizabeth held her breath and stood perfectly still. The sound repeated itself. Elizabeth's heart began pounding in her chest. She took a deep breath, trying to calm the sound of her heart.

"Liz," came a low voice. Elizabeth looked in the direction of the sound. But all she saw was a big pile of tree branches. Suddenly a head popped out. It was Joey.

Joey motioned her into his hiding place. Lifting up the tree branches, he ushered her down into the ground. Elizabeth climbed in quickly and looked around. They were in some sort of underground cave about five feet across. It was like a secret fortress hidden in the earth.

"Joey," Elizabeth said, her voice wavering.

Joey looked deep into her eyes and wrapped her in his arms. "Oh, Liz, I've missed you," he said. Elizabeth hugged him back, feeling her heart well with emotion.

Then she leaned back to look in his eyes. "I thought you hated me," she said softly.

"I was hurt at first," Joey whispered. "But then I realized that you were in an awkward situation. I've been watching the two of you. I can tell you don't really love Todd." Joey stared in her eyes. "Tell him it's over," he urged.

Elizabeth nodded mutely. With the sound of other voices in the distance, he leaned in and kissed her.

As soon as Joey's lips left hers the branches parted above them. Startled, they jumped apart. A penlight shone into their faces. Elizabeth blinked at the light.

"Found you!" Todd said cheerfully, climbing down into the hiding place. "Is there room in here for three?"

Joey and Elizabeth nodded wordlessly.

Todd inched in next to Elizabeth and put an arm around her. "I knew I would find you," he whispered in her ear. "My instincts take me right to you."

Elizabeth's heart sank—how could she hurt Todd? But then, how could she fight her feelings for Joey?

In the darkness, Joey's eyes burned into hers.

# Chapter 5

*Brring. Brring.* A faint sound disturbed Elizabeth at five A.M. on Wednesday morning. She pulled the sheet over her head and snuggled down in her covers. But then the annoying sound repeated itself. Kicking off the sheet, Elizabeth opened her eyes and tried to place the noise. It was the alarm clock. She pressed the button groggily and looked around her, feeling disoriented.

She was in the female junior counselors' cabin. Todd had to leave early this morning, and Elizabeth was getting up to say good-bye—forever. Elizabeth stretched and rubbed her eyes. Her whole body ached. She felt like she hadn't slept at all the whole night. She had tossed and turned for hours, trying to decide how to break the news to Todd.

Elizabeth slid out of bed, her stomach tight with anticipation. She looked over at Nicole's bed. Nicole was sleeping peacefully, a slight smile on her face.

*That figures,* Elizabeth thought. *She even looks crafty in her sleep. She's probably plotting something in her dreams.* Although Todd was leaving in a few hours, Elizabeth would be nervous until he actually got into his car and drove away. She couldn't believe Nicole hadn't gotten involved yet. Elizabeth was sure Nicole had something up her sleeve.

Pulling on shorts and a T-shirt, Elizabeth crept out of the sleeping cabin. She paused as she entered the forest, feeling a moment of wonder. The woods were quiet and damp at this hour of the morning. Crickets were clicking in the brush and birds were chirping high in the trees.

Elizabeth felt a sense of peace wash over her as she walked through the quiet woods. *It's going to be all right,* she told herself. *Todd will understand. Just tell him that it's not working out anymore, that things are different now—that you've met another guy.* Elizabeth bit her lip. Todd wouldn't understand. Todd would be devastated.

When she reached the activities cabins, Elizabeth walked out of the woods and headed down to the lake. She and Todd had decided to meet in front of the dock, at the patch of beach where she had taken him his first day there. "At our place," he had said.

As she rounded the corner of the boathouse she caught sight of Todd. He was sitting in the sand, his knees hugged up to his chest. His profile was perfectly outlined in the morning light, and he looked pensive. For a moment Elizabeth's breath caught in her throat. She had almost forgotten how handsome Todd was.

Then, as if he sensed her eyes on him, he turned and saw her standing there. "Liz." He smiled.

"Morning," Elizabeth said, crossing the sand and joining him.

"Good morning, sunshine," Todd said.

Elizabeth laughed and made a face. "Todd, sometimes you can be so dorky."

"And sometimes you can be so conceited," Todd returned. "I wasn't talking about you."

Elizabeth looked at him quizzically.

"See?" Todd said, pointing to the horizon.

Elizabeth sucked in her breath as she took in the splendid scene in front of her. The lake was a calm pale blue and the sun was a golden orb just peeking over the horizon.

Pulling her back against him, Todd wrapped his arms around her waist. Elizabeth leaned back against his chest, and they watched the sunrise together. The sun rose in a glorious burst of orange and yellow, sending a shaft of shimmering gold across the placid lake.

"Oh, Todd, it's beautiful," Elizabeth breathed.

"It's even better than Miller's Point, isn't it?" Todd asked. Miller's Point was a popular parking spot overlooking Sweet Valley. It was Elizabeth and Todd's favorite place to go when they wanted to have some time alone together.

Suddenly her whole life with Todd came flooding back to her. Places jumped into her mind: Miller's Point, where they kissed for hours late at night; the Dairi Burger, where they met their friends for a burger and shake after a game; the basketball stadium, where she watched Todd play; the *Oracle* office, where Todd always stopped by for a chat. Random memories returned to her: their first kiss under their favorite tree in the park, the first time she had watched Todd play basketball, the first time Elizabeth had shown him a story she had written. . . .

Todd was Elizabeth's constant companion at Sweet Valley. He shared all her experiences with her, and he was always there when she needed him. Sweet Valley wouldn't be the same without him.

Shaking her head hard, Elizabeth pushed the thoughts away. She wasn't at Sweet Valley. She was in the mountains of Montana, and she was in love with another boy. She had to be fair to Todd and tell him the truth. And she had to tell him now.

"Todd—," Elizabeth began, but he pulled her to him and kissed her passionately. Elizabeth resisted at first, but then she felt herself responding to his kiss. It felt like coming home again. She wrapped her arms around his neck and kissed him with a fervor she didn't know she felt.

When he pulled away, she was breathless.

Todd sat back on his heels and gave her a tender look. He gently brushed back a lock of her golden hair from her cheek. "I don't know if it's the mountain air or what, but over the last couple of days I've fallen in love with you all over again," he said.

Elizabeth looked into Todd's warm brown eyes and her heart melted. She decided she did love Todd—definitely. Right? She put her arms around him and kissed him again. "I've fallen in love all over again, too," she said softly.

   ❖     ❖     ❖

"And step and step and turn!" Jessica called, sliding to the right and spinning around. Jessica was at the dance studio on Wednesday morning, teaching the girls a funky hip-hop line dance. Today she had her own group of campers for the dance workshop, and they were thrilled about it.

"Yabadee doo bop bop," Jessica sang as the song came to an end and the last beats of the music sounded. As a grand finale Jessica shimmied and shook her hips. The girls laughed gleefully and shook their hips as well, mimicking her exactly. Jessica smiled as she looked in the wall-length mirror at the line of little girls behind her. They looked adorable. They were all wearing pink tights and leotards and little ballet slippers. Sofia and her sister had on little black gauze skirts over their tights.

"OK, let's take it from the top," Jessica instructed, rewinding the tape and standing with her hands on her hips. The campers quickly followed. At the count of four Jessica started moving to the right. "One-two-three-four, one-two-three-four," she directed. "And step and step—"

"And turn!" the girls yelled out, pirouetting wildly. They liked turning best. The only problem was that Jessica couldn't seem to get them to stop at one rotation. Once they started turning, they just kept on going. Jessica stopped the tape and took in the roomful of girls spinning around wildly, their arms spread out at their sides. Sofia and Anastasia's skirts whirled out to their sides.

"Whoa!" Stephanie said as she collided with Sarah.

"I'm dizzy!" Sofia exclaimed, collapsing to the wooden floor.

"Me too!" her sister said, falling down next to her.

"OK, why don't we take a break?" Jessica suggested as soon as they all had spun to a stop. "If you want, you can sit down and have some water. And if you're feeling inspired, you can work on some of the dance steps."

"I want to pwactice," Stephanie said, pulling Sarah up.

"Me too!" Maggie cried, jumping up to join them.

Holding hands in a line, the girls started working on the routine on their own, prancing across the floor while they sang out the words to the song. "Yabadee doo bop bop!" yelled out Stephanie, bumping hips with Sarah and Maggie.

Anastasia knelt beside Sofia and began braiding her little sister's dark, satiny hair. Tanya plopped down on the floor against the wall, a water bottle in her hand.

Jessica sat down next to her. She was hoping to find out if Paul would be coming to the camp again anytime soon.

"Jessica, when do I get to be you for a day?" Tanya asked.

"Whenever you like," Jessica replied.

"Do I really get to be you for the *whole* day?" Tanya asked.

Jessica nodded, and Tanya clapped excitedly.

"Can I be you today?" Tanya asked. "I brought my costume with me."

"Well, let's see what you've got," Jessica said.

Tanya unzipped her gym bag and dumped the contents on the wooden floor. Then she wriggled into her outfit, a floral slit skirt and a little crop top. She slipped her feet into leather sandals and pushed her sunglasses up on her forehead. Fluffing her hair out over her shoulders, she put her hand on her side, jutting out one hip. "Well, do I look like you?"

"I don't know," Jessica said, sizing up the little girl. "Something's missing."

Tanya looked at her eagerly. "What?"

Jessica pondered for a minute. "Purple. That's it. You need to wear something purple."

Tanya's face fell. "But I don't have anything purple." Then her eyes lit up. "I know! I have a purple sweatshirt at home!"

Jessica pounced on the opportunity. "Maybe you should call your brother and have him drop it by," she suggested.

"That's a good idea!" Tanya breathed.

"But don't tell him the real reason why," Jessica warned. "He would think it's silly." Jessica spoke in a conspiratorial tone. "You know how boys are. They don't understand anything."

"They don't understand anything!" Tanya burst out rapturously.

Jessica's mind was clicking. "I know. I have a plan," she said. She leaned in close. "Tell him it's been cold at night and you don't want to get sick."

Tanya giggled gleefully. "Can I call him now?"

Jessica nodded. "But come right back." Tanya jumped up and ran to the door.

Jessica watched her go, looking after her with satisfaction. Her plan was in motion. As soon as Paul got there Jessica was going to waylay him. Jessica rubbed her hands together excitedly. Once he saw her, there was no way he'd be able to resist her charms.

"Bye, Liz," Todd said, squeezing her in his arms.

"Bye, Todd," Elizabeth responded, hugging him tightly back. "Take care of yourself."

Todd drew back from their embrace and touched her cheek lightly. "Be good," he said.

Elizabeth winced and looked away. She'd try.

It was mid-morning and Todd and Elizabeth were in the parking lot in the midst of the many campers who wanted to see Todd off. It looked like Todd had made himself popular in the few days he had been at the camp. Aaron and Winston were there with their groups of campers, too.

Winston patted Todd on his back. "Have a good trip, man."

Elizabeth did a double take when she saw Winston. He was wearing a straw hat and cowboy boots, and he seemed to be walking with some difficulty.

"Hey, Winston, nice look," Elizabeth teased.

Winston shook his head, a mournful expression on his face. "Don't ask."

"Remember, man," Todd said cryptically to Winston. "Don't give up."

Elizabeth looked at them curiously. Something was definitely going on with the guys.

"Don't worry, Todd," Aaron said. "I'll make sure of it."

81

Winston looked pained. "Todd, do you think you could take him with you?"

Just then a little boy ran through the group and made a pistol with his fist. "Bang bang bang bang!" he cried.

"You missed me, Jacob," Todd said, pointing an imaginary arrow at the boy. "Ping!"

"Bang bang!" the boy returned.

"Ow! You got me!" Todd cried, pretending to be wounded and staggering to the ground. Grabbing his hand to his heart, he fell flat on his back on the asphalt. The boys laughed at Todd's dramatic display.

"OK, that's it for the comedy show," Todd said, picking himself up and looking at his watch. "I've got to take off. If I don't get back by early evening, the coach will kill me."

He gave Elizabeth a kiss on the cheek and jumped into the front seat of his car. Catching Elizabeth's eye in the rearview mirror, he smiled and waved. The campers waved after him.

As the taillights of Todd's BMW faded away into the distance, Elizabeth breathed a sigh of relief. She couldn't believe she made it through his whole visit without him finding out about Joey. Now that she was on her own again, she had some major decisions to make. And they wouldn't be easy.

# Chapter 6

"Earth to Elizabeth!" Rose called, waving a hand in front of her face. It was Wednesday afternoon, and Elizabeth was out on the dock with Rose and a group of fifteen-year-old girls. Rose was giving the girls an introductory sailing seminar before they went out on the lake later that afternoon.

"Huh?" Elizabeth asked, startled.

"I asked you if you could get some ropes from the boathouse," Rose repeated, sounding irritated. Some of the girls snickered.

"You want some boats from the rope house?" Elizabeth repeated, trying to digest the words. "I mean, ropes from the boathouse?"

Now Rose looked at her in concern. "Are you all right?" she asked. She laid a hand on Elizabeth's forehead. "Maybe you've gotten sunstroke."

"No, Rose, I'm fine," Elizabeth said, standing up and pulling on her beach cover-up over her bathing suit. Actually she did feel a little dizzy. It was a clear, hot day and the sun was beating down relentlessly on her back. "I'll go get the ropes."

Elizabeth grabbed her sandals from the dock and rushed off, feeling totally humiliated. She could feel the eyes of the girls on her. *No wonder they call me Dizzy Lizzie,* Elizabeth thought in disgust. She'd been a total space case ever since she'd gotten to camp.

And today was no exception. Elizabeth had been in a daze all day, trying to work out her conflicting feelings. She couldn't believe that she had reaffirmed her feelings for Todd just when she meant to break up with him. She felt like she wasn't in control of her own life. It was as if she was just letting the tide of circumstance carry her along.

Elizabeth wanted to kick herself. *How did I let myself get in such a sticky situation?* This was the way Jessica led her life, not the way Elizabeth usually did. Elizabeth always knew what she wanted, and she always let her morals guide her. But now—now she did whatever felt right at the moment.

Elizabeth paused and slipped on her sandals, feeling lower than the lowest sea amoeba. She was racked with guilt. First she lied to Joey about Todd, and then she lied to Todd about Joey. *Joey, Todd, Joey, Todd.* The names swirled in her mind. Elizabeth couldn't seem to decide between them.

Elizabeth pushed open the door of the boathouse. It was dark and cool inside. Elizabeth sat down on an upside-down canoe, deep in thought. She could hear someone rummaging through the supply shed in back. Moments later Maria's head popped up.

"Maria!" Elizabeth exclaimed, glad to see her close friend. If there was anyone who could help her with her dilemma, it was Maria. Maria could always be counted on to be calm and levelheaded.

"Hey, Liz," Maria said, carrying an armful of different-size oars across the room and plopping them down on the ground. "Whew!" she said, wiping her brow. "Getting props can be a difficult job."

Maria knelt on the ground and wrapped a thick piece of twine around the oars. "So what's up? It looks like you could use an ear."

"I could use a brain," Elizabeth said woefully.

"You have a brain," Maria pointed out. "You just have to use it."

"I know," Elizabeth said.

Maria tied the rope in a knot and jumped up on the canoe next to Elizabeth. "So how did it go this morning? Did Todd take the news OK?"

Elizabeth shook her head.

"Oh no," Maria said. "Was he devastated?"

Elizabeth shook her head again. "Not exactly," she confessed, feeling embarrassed. "I didn't tell him."

"You didn't tell him!" Maria exclaimed. "But why not?"

"Maria, I don't know what happened," Elizabeth whined. "I was all set to break up with him when suddenly I fell in love with him all over again."

"Uh-oh," Maria said. "You're beginning to sound like your sister."

"I think I'm *becoming* my sister," Elizabeth agreed. Then she looked at Maria with thoughtful eyes. "Do you think it's possible to be in love with two guys at one time?"

Maria frowned. "I don't really think so. It seems to me that one case would be love and the other infatuation."

"Well, in that case Todd is love and Joey's an infatuation," Elizabeth reasoned. "I'm obviously meant to be with Todd. Todd's for good. Joey's just for the moment."

Elizabeth contemplated giving up Joey and felt a stabbing pain in her heart. She shook her head. "Maria, rationalizing it doesn't work. The idea of giving Joey up is too painful to think about."

"Maybe that means you don't really love Todd anymore," Maria suggested.

"Yeah, maybe I'm just afraid to give up the security of a boyfriend," Elizabeth agreed.

Elizabeth tried to imagine what it would be like at Sweet Valley High without a relationship with Todd. She had a full life, with lots of friends and lots of activities. Maybe it would be OK after all. But when she tried to imagine it, all she could picture was a long empty corridor. She was overcome with such a sense of sadness that it threatened to overwhelm her.

Elizabeth put her head in her hands. "Maria, there's no use fighting it. I'm definitely in love with two guys at once. I just can't give up either one."

"Liz, you've got to," Maria insisted. "It's not fair to Todd or Joey—or yourself."

Elizabeth shrugged. "I can't." She hopped off the canoe and grabbed a huge coil of rope from the wall. "Well, there's no reason for anyone to suffer," she decided, slinging the rope over her shoulder. "I'll just keep my summer affair a secret. Todd will never have to know what happened between me and Joey. As soon as camp is over, I'll never see Joey again."

Maria slid off the canoe and picked up her pile of oars. "I think you're making a mistake," she warned.

Elizabeth pushed open the door and they walked out into the sunlight. "After all, if Jessica is going to act like me, then I might as well act like Jessica. Right?" Elizabeth said lightly.

"Wrong," Maria said firmly.

"You'll see, Maria, it'll all work out in the end," Elizabeth insisted.

But Maria shook her head. "Girl, you're heading for trouble."

Elizabeth whistled as she made her way through the woods after her sailing workshop. She was heading back to the JC cabin to freshen up before dinner. Now that she had made her decision, her spirits were much higher. She couldn't wait to see Joey. All she had to do at this point was figure out how to explain the situation to him.

Obviously she couldn't tell him the truth. Maria was naive to think Joey would understand. He would have no interest in a romance with her if he knew she was in love with another boy at the same time. And he certainly wouldn't appreciate the idea of serving as a temporary boyfriend while Elizabeth was here at camp.

She would have to tell him she had broken up with Todd. But how could she explain why their summer romance had to be kept a secret? Then it hit her. She would tell Joey that she didn't want to hurt Todd. Todd's friends were all at camp, and it would be painful for him to know she'd gotten involved with someone else so quickly.

A pang of guilt hit her, but then she pushed it away. After all, she'd been lying for so long, why stop now?

Whistling softly, Elizabeth swung open the cabin door and headed for her bunk. Then she stood stock-still. Nicole was lounging on her bed, flipping through an anthology of English literature.

Elizabeth turned to walk right out, but Nicole stood up quickly and blocked the door.

"I think we need to have a little chat," Nicole declared.

Elizabeth crossed her hands over her chest. "We don't have anything to talk about," she said coldly.

"What, are you afraid I'll spill the beans?" Nicole challenged her.

"I'm simply not interested in anything you have to say," Elizabeth returned. "So if you don't mind getting out of my way—"

"Because I will, you know," Nicole threatened, her eyes glittering evilly.

Elizabeth sat down hard on her bunk. She had been expecting this. She knew Nicole wouldn't pass up a chance to blackmail her. She just hoped the stakes wouldn't be too high. "Fine, go ahead and say what you have to say."

Nicole laughed softly and let the door swing shut. She picked up her book and held it in the air.

"Actually I just wanted to read you a bit from Sir Walter Scott." Smiling sweetly at Elizabeth, she ran her finger down the page. "Aha, here it is!" She cleared her throat and quoted in a loud, dramatic voice. "'Oh, what a tangled web we weave / When first we practice to deceive.'"

Elizabeth could feel the blood rush to her face. She was embarrassed and she was outraged. How dare Nicole accuse her of being deceitful? Nicole was the most hypocritical girl Elizabeth had ever met. "I think he wrote those lines for you," she said angrily.

Nicole turned wide eyes to Elizabeth. "For *me*? *I'm* not the one seeing two guys at the same time."

Elizabeth was getting fed up. "Nicole, would you just get to the point?"

"Fine," Nicole said, slamming the book shut and taking a seat on the edge of her bunk across from Elizabeth. She turned cold, hard eyes to Elizabeth. "I want you to do two things for me."

Elizabeth waited in silent apprehension.

"*First* I want you to cut things off with Joey." She paused to let the words sink in. "And *then* I want you to put in a good word for me."

"And if I decide not to?" Elizabeth asked, fire in her eyes.

Nicole shrugged. "Then you'll suffer the consequences. It's your choice. As long as you quit seeing lover boy, then I'll keep my mouth shut. Otherwise, Todd's going to hear a very interesting story."

Elizabeth smirked. "Sorry, it's too late for that," she said. "Todd's already gone. He left this morning."

"Well, then, I'll just have to write him a letter,"

Nicole said. "It's a good thing I found your address book lying around in the cabin."

Elizabeth's mouth dropped open. Nicole would stop at nothing. "Don't you have any shame?"

Nicole looked at her wide eyed. "Well, the book was lying open on your bed. The address just jumped out at me." She pulled her marker out of her book and waved it under Elizabeth's nose. Something was scribbled on it. "And I just happened to copy it down." Nicole put the bookmark in the back pocket of her jeans and patted it. "I've got it right here. Just in case I need it."

Elizabeth felt like kicking herself. She should have known better than to leave her address book lying around in the cabin.

Nicole stood up and tapped her foot. "So what's your answer?" she asked, looking at Elizabeth through narrowed eyes. "Do you want to have a chat with Joey?"

Elizabeth's heart sank. Nicole had her over a barrel, and she knew it. Elizabeth thought about Joey and his passionate kisses. Then she thought about Todd and his warm, steady loyalty.

Elizabeth nodded silently. Nicole had won.

"Jennifer, get your fingers out of your food!" Elizabeth instructed that night at dinner in the cafeteria. Jennifer looked up guiltily and dropped her string beans back on her plate. She was a messy girl whose clothes were always in disarray.

Elizabeth shook her head in disgust. "Didn't your parents teach you any manners?"

Jennifer reddened and picked up her fork.

"Oh, this is gross," Adrienne said in a sniveling voice. She pushed around the stir-fried vegetables on her plate.

"If I hear one more complaint out of you, I'm going to report you to Lacey," Elizabeth threatened. "Bernard spends hours preparing well-balanced meals so you can get the energy you need, and all you can do is whine."

Adrienne and Jennifer exchanged worried looks. The rest of the girls turned back to their meals, eating their food in silence.

"Elizabeth, is something wrong?" Aimee ventured in a timid voice.

"No, nothing's wrong!" Elizabeth responded sharply. "Can't you just let me eat in peace?"

At Elizabeth's harsh tone, Maria twisted around in her seat and looked at her in surprise. She was sitting with her campers at the next table. "You OK?" she mouthed to Elizabeth.

Elizabeth nodded silently and looked down, feeling ashamed of her outburst. She stabbed at her food and brought a forkful of vegetables to her mouth. Her mouth was dry, and she almost gagged. Swallowing a mouthful of water, she forced down the food. She stole a look across the cafeteria to where Jocy was eating. He looked adorable as usual as he joked around with his campers.

Elizabeth felt a tap on her shoulder and looked up. It was Maria. "I'm thirsty," she said. "Let's go get a drink of water."

"Good idea," Elizabeth agreed quickly. She

dropped her napkin on the table and followed Maria to the water fountain. They could still keep an eye on their campers from the fountain in the corner.

Maria pushed the button and took a drink of water. "So," she said when she straightened up. "Are you trying to be Lacey tonight?"

Elizabeth sighed. "It looks that way, doesn't it? I know I'm not being fair. I'm in a horrible mood and I'm taking it out on my campers. I can't seem to help myself."

"Well, for Elizabeth Wakefield to lose her sunny demeanor, something drastic must have occurred," Maria reasoned.

Elizabeth nodded. "It did."

Maria looked at her, a question in her eyes.

Elizabeth hesitated. She wanted more than anything to confide in Maria, but Maria was still friends with Nicole. "Listen, Maria, if I tell you something, will you promise not to tell anyone?"

"Of course not—you know me," Maria reassured.

Elizabeth nodded. She knew she could trust Maria. Elizabeth searched the room carefully. Nicole was occupied with her campers at a far table. Lowering her voice, Elizabeth recounted the scene in the cabin.

Maria sucked in her breath. "Nicole's blackmailing you!"

Elizabeth nodded grimly.

Maria shook her head. "I don't know what's gotten into that girl."

"Nothing's gotten into her," Elizabeth said. "She's just revealing her true personality."

But Maria shook her head thoughtfully. "I don't know," she said slowly. "Something doesn't quite fit." Then she turned sympathetic eyes to Elizabeth. "So what are you going to do?"

"I've got to break the news to Joey now, so Nicole can witness the encounter. Joey's going to hate me. And if I don't talk to Joey, my relationship with Todd will be over." Elizabeth sighed. "Either way, I'm doomed."

"I guess you don't really have a choice, do you?" Maria asked.

"Not really," Elizabeth said. Then she stood up straighter. "Well, I might as well get it over now before I lose my courage altogether."

"Good luck," Maria said, giving her hand a squeeze.

Elizabeth smiled at her gratefully. Then she marched across the noisy cafeteria and headed for Joey's table.

Joey's eyes lit up when he saw her. "Elizabeth!" he exclaimed.

Elizabeth couldn't meet his eyes. "Joey, I, uh—" Her stomach churned at the thought of what she was about to say, and she hesitated. She didn't know if she could go through with it. Then she felt Nicole's eyes boring into her from across the room. She had to do it.

"Joey, we have to talk," she said.

"Sure, Liz," Joey said, looking at her in concern. "Have a seat." He patted the bench next to him.

Elizabeth sat down and took a deep breath. "I think I made a mistake." Then she rushed ahead before she could stop herself. "My affair with you was just a summer fling. I don't really care for you after all."

"What?" Joey exclaimed. "But I thought—"

Elizabeth cut him off. "Since Todd visited, I realized that I love Todd and only Todd." Then she closed her eyes. This was the hardest part. "I think you'd be much happier with Nicole."

Joey paled visibly and tears welled up in his eyes.

Elizabeth saw Nicole staring at her from across the room. Feeling sick, she forced herself to get up and walk away from the table.

Elizabeth headed back to her table, blinking back tears. She hadn't realized what a good actress she could be.

"Liz, are you all right?" Maria asked with concern as Elizabeth sat down with her campers.

"Just fine," Elizabeth said glumly, her eyes glued on Joey's table. She watched with despair as Nicole plopped down next to Joey with a friendly smile. Elizabeth felt as though a knife were twisting slowly in her gut.

Maria leaned over and patted Elizabeth sympathetically on the back.

"Mmm, I love caviar," Lila said, spreading a spoonful of black fish eggs onto a piece of thick, soft bread and popping it into her mouth. It was ten P.M. on Wednesday night, and Lila and Bo were sharing a late night snack on the dock. They'd had it delivered express mail from the Gourmet Grocery in Sweet Valley.

"Me too," Bo agreed, leaning in for a quick kiss. "It's salty and sweet—just like you." He gave her a sexy smile, with one side of his mouth higher than the other. Bo's crooked smile always made Lila's stomach flutter. In fact, everything about Bo made her stomach flutter—from his brown curly hair to his deep brown eyes to his tanned, masculine build.

Lila looked appreciatively at the spread laid out before them. *The Gourmet Grocery really outdid themselves this time,* she thought contentedly. They had an elaborate meal of baguettes and Brie cheese, smoked salmon, grape leaves, and little pastry puffs. The gourmet shop had even sent a miniature bottle of sparkling apple cider along with two wineglasses.

They had received their package at mail call after lunch. Lacey had not been pleased when she'd seen it. She had lifted an eyebrow and had given them a funny look. "Express mail to camp," she had said disapprovingly. "How *unusual.*"

"Do you remember Lacey's expression when she saw the package?" Lila asked.

Bo laughed. "I thought she was going to explode."

Lila tore off a hunk of bread and spread warm Brie cheese on it. She sank her teeth into it ravenously. "I thought I'd never see real food again," she said.

"Me either," Bo echoed, popping a pastry puff into his mouth. "I'm getting a little sick of grilled cheese and bug juice."

"And tree bark tea," Lila added. They both laughed at the memory. When Lila had been trying to convince Bo that she was a wilderness woman, she had learned to make tea from tree bark. Bo had pretended that he loved it and actually had drunk a few cups of the nasty stuff.

After they'd finished the food and drunk down the last drop of apple cider, they swept the garbage into a bag and stood up.

"How about a moonlight walk on the beach?" Bo suggested.

Hand in hand they walked along the water's edge. The lake was a placid green, and the sky was a velvety midnight blue twinkling with stars.

"If you could wish for something, what would it be?" Bo asked, putting an arm around her and drawing her close to him.

"Let's see," Lila said, her brown eyes twinkling mischievously. "A four-poster bed, a duvet cover, Million-Dollar mocha ice cream, a private jet—"

"Lila Fowler!" Bo interrupted. "Don't you have any nonmaterialistic dreams?"

Lila crossed her arms over her chest. "Humph! What did you have in mind?"

"Oh, I don't know," Bo said. "World peace, winning the Olympics—something like that."

"Well, I think my wishes are much more realistic." Lila pouted.

"Actually, if I could have any wish come true, do you know what it would be?" Bo asked, his brown eyes gleaming brightly.

Lila shook her head.

Bo pulled her down in the sand and took her in his arms. "You," he said in a soft, husky voice.

Lila leaned in to kiss him. "But you've got me."

"I know," Bo said. "But now that I've found you, I never want to lose you again."

Lila put a finger to his lips. "Shh," she said. "Let's not talk about it. We've still got over two weeks to be together at camp."

Bo looked deep into her eyes and Lila could feel her stomach jump. She lifted her face up to his, closing her eyes as his warm lips met hers.

# Chapter 7

Winston was brooding by the lake Thursday afternoon after his tumbling workshop. He'd gotten another "Hank" letter from Maria. Winston was outfitted in full cowboy attire, and he was baking in the late afternoon sun. He pulled off his oversize boots and threw them on the dock. Then he rolled up his jeans and let his feet dangle in the water.

Winston pulled the letter out of his jeans pocket and read through it again.

> *My grandma's got real cattle on the ranch—and pigs and horses. . . . Today Hank taught me how to lasso the horns of a real live steer (!). I never thought I'd like life on a ranch so much. Maybe I'll never come back (ha, ha).*
>
> *Maria*

Winston violently ripped up the letter and dropped it on the dock, feeling as if he'd been burned. "Maybe I'll never come back," Maria had written. Winston wasn't stupid. He could read between the lines. Maria was so in love with her cowboy that she didn't want to leave him. She'd probably marry him and live out her days in the old West, riding bareback and raising cattle.

And she hadn't even written *love* at the end of the letter. No "take care" or "yours truly." She might as well have written "Your friend, Maria."

Winston scowled. The least Maria could do was tell him directly that it was over between them. She didn't have to keep sending him little hints. Picking up the pieces of the letter, Winston stood up and flung them far out in the lake. He watched them slowly float away, feeling as if it were Maria drifting away from him.

Totally dejected, he sat back down on the dock and dropped his head into his hands.

Then his friends' words came back to him. "Are you just going to give up?" Todd had asked. "Doesn't Maria mean anything to you?" Aaron had added.

Winston sat up with newfound determination. Maybe Maria was interested in another guy, but Winston wasn't going to let her go so easily. Todd and Aaron were right. A guy had to fight for what he wanted. If Maria wanted a cowboy, then she was going to get one. Winston jumped up and ran into the boathouse.

"Jessica, Jessica, look what I made!" Tanya cried, waving a picture in the air as she came running out of arts and crafts on Thursday afternoon. Jessica was waiting for her in front of the arts cabin.

Jessica took the sheet of construction paper from the girl's outstretched hand. It was some kind of abstract finger painting. Swirls of bright fuschia and purple covered the page. Jessica furrowed her brow, trying to make out the image.

"See? That's a house, and that's a girl!" Tanya exclaimed. "And that's a cow in the sky!" She pointed to the page with a bright pink finger.

"Wow, Tanya, you're really talented," Jessica enthused. "Maybe you'll be a famous modern painter someday."

Tanya beamed at Jessica's praise. "No, I want to be an actress," she said. "Just like you!"

Jessica smiled and took the girl's hand. "Where are you meeting your brother?" she asked. Paul was scheduled to come to the camp that afternoon to drop off Tanya's sweatshirt.

"In front of the boathouse," Tanya answered.

"OK, let's go wait for him," Jessica said, turning onto the little dirt path that led to the lake. Tanya skipped along beside her, holding her hand tight.

Jessica's mind clicked as they walked along the path. She needed to get Paul alone. And she needed to make sure he couldn't get away.

"There's the boathouse!" Tanya exclaimed, pointing to the wooden structure ahead of them. "I love boats! Yesterday we went sailing and tomorrow we're going canoeing!"

Jessica's eyes lit up. Canoeing! That was just the thing. If she could get Paul to go canoeing with her on the lake, then he wouldn't have any means of escape. Jessica's eyes darted mischievously as she came up with a plan. She was going to have to trick Paul into getting into a canoe. All she needed was a little help from Tanya.

When they reached the boathouse, Jessica knelt and faced the little girl. "Tanya, can you keep a secret?" she asked.

Tanya turned wide eyes to her and nodded eagerly. "I *love* secrets."

"I need to talk to Paul alone for a few minutes, but you can't tell him," she explained.

"Paul won't talk to you," Tanya said. "Paul hates girls."

"That's just the problem," Jessica said. "That's why I need your help."

"We have to trick him!" Tanya exclaimed, sounding thrilled at the idea.

"Exactly," Jessica said. She lowered her voice to a whisper. "Here's the plan. You've got to tell Paul that you need to talk to him privately. In a canoe. Then I'll jump in instead of you."

Tanya nodded. Suddenly they heard the sound of an engine rumbling along the road leading to the main lodge.

"That must be him!" Tanya exclaimed.

"OK, go out in the water," Jessica instructed. "I'll be hiding in the boathouse." Tanya peeled off her clothes and ran into the water in her bathing suit.

Jessica watched from the window of the boathouse as Paul strolled casually across the sand, Tanya's sweatshirt flung over his arm. Her stomach fluttered at the sight of him. He was wearing black jeans and a faded blue cotton shirt. His black wavy hair peeked out of a white painter's cap.

"Paul, Paul, here I am!" Tanya called from the lake, where she was treading water.

Paul walked out on the dock and knelt. "Do you want this or should I throw it in the water?" he called out to his sister.

Tanya swam a few feet until she reached a canoe tied up to the dock. Holding on to the edge, she kicked out her feet and floated in the water. "Can we take a canoe out together?" she asked. "I really need to talk to you privately."

Paul rolled his eyes, obviously irritated with his sister. "Can't we talk here on the dock?"

"Oh, Paul, please?" Tanya implored, turning big brown eyes to him.

Paul sighed. He dropped the sweatshirt on the pier and climbed into the canoe. Unwrapping the rope from the dock, he picked up an oar. "Get in," he said.

But suddenly Jessica ran to the dock and eased herself into the canoe with him. "Tanya, do you mind if I talk to Paul alone for a minute?"

"OK," Tanya said. She hoisted herself onto the dock and climbed out of the water. Grabbing the sweatshirt off the pier, she ran to the shore.

"What? You!" Paul exclaimed, glaring at Jessica. "Didn't you get my note?"

Jessica nodded and smiled sweetly. "That's why I'm here." She picked up an oar and started paddling. "I decided I had to kidnap you."

Paul glowered at her. Tanya giggled and waved from the shore.

Winston stood on the dock and flung a rope out into the water, trying to lasso the anchor of a boat. The rope landed a foot short and bounced along the choppy water. He wound it up and tried to swing it in an arc, but it was impossible to maneuver the wet twine. He threw the heavy rope aside and picked up another coil. Swinging his arm in a big circle, he took aim and hurled the second rope far out into the water. This time it settled on the anchor and held tight.

Winston stared at it for a moment in shock. *I've actually done it. This isn't so hard after all.*

Feeling encouraged, Winston pulled at the taut rope until the knot gave way. He reeled in the rope and threw it aside. Kicking aside the wet cords by his feet, he reached for a dry coil. Cocking his hip arrogantly, he swung the rope in a wide arc around his right arm and scanned the water for a new target.

"Hey, you want to lasso me?" a sultry voice asked.

Winston jumped at the sound of Lara's voice. He turned to see her walking onto the dock, wearing an orange bikini. Her sunglasses were propped up on her head, holding back her mass of wild red curly hair, and a straw bag was slung over one arm. Winston's eyes almost popped out of his head. The rope tangled around his legs and he tripped to the dock.

"While you're down there, do you think you can help me with my sunscreen?" Lara asked in a laughing voice.

Winston gulped as Lara spread out her towel and lay down on her stomach.

"Uh, sure," he said. Untangling the rope from his legs, he knelt beside her.

Propping herself up on an elbow, Lara fished around in her bag and pulled out a bottle of suntan lotion. "Here you go," she said, handing him the container. "And please be careful to get every spot. I've got *very* sensitive skin." Lara settled back down, resting her forehead on her hands.

As Winston smoothed the lotion on her delicate white skin, he bit his lip. It was hard to remember that Lara was just a camper. He forced himself to feel miserable about Maria.

"So do you want to go in the direction of the boys' cabins or the girls' cabins?" Jessica asked, flashing Paul a big smile.

Paul didn't answer. Crossing his arms across his chest, he leaned back against the seat and put on his sunglasses. Ever since she had abducted him, Paul had been fuming silently. He refused to talk to her, and he refused to help her paddle.

"Neither, huh?" Jessica said. "I guess we'll go out in the middle of the lake, then." Jessica grunted as she pushed the oar deep into the water and got the canoe moving again. Shifting from the left to the right as she paddled, she managed to cut a crooked path across the lake.

"Phew," Jessica said when they reached the middle of the lake. She picked up a towel and wiped off her forehead. Paul's legs were stretched out in the canoe and his arms were flung over the side. His eyes were closed, and he looked like he was enjoying the afternoon sun. Jessica put down the oar and let the canoe drift.

"So, tell me about Celia," she said.

Paul's eyes flew open. "Celia who?" he asked, narrowing his eyes.

"There's no use playing dumb," Jessica said. "I already know the whole story."

Paul shrugged. "There's nothing to know—it's ancient history."

"Well, if it's ancient history, you don't seem to be over it," Jessica pointed out.

"How would you know?" Paul asked.

"It's obvious. You don't want to get involved with me because you're afraid you'll get hurt again," Jessica said.

Paul laughed harshly. "Don't flatter yourself, Jessica. I don't want to see you because of the reason I stated in my note. That's all there is to it."

Jessica moved in closer and looked him straight in the eyes. "Paul Mathis, I think you're a coward."

"That has nothing to do with it," Paul said hotly. "You just don't understand."

"I understand more than you realize," Jessica said softly. Then she decided to tell him about Christian. Paul was never going to open up to her unless she opened up to him first. But she was going to have to give him an edited version of the story. Paul would never trust her if he knew she'd cheated on Ken with Christian.

"I . . . I was going out with this guy for a while.

His name was Christian, and he was a surfer. We went surfing together every morning at five A.M." Jessica glanced at Paul. He had a skeptical look on his face, but he was listening.

Feeling vulnerable, Jessica forced herself to go on. "It was a complicated situation. Some of the guys in my school had formed a gang, and Christian was the leader of the rival gang. One day the two gangs got in a fight at a party, and Christian died in an accident in the pool." Jessica was trying to recount the story objectively, but her voice choked up.

For a moment it looked like she'd gotten Paul's defenses down. Paul took Jessica's hand and pulled her toward him in a hug. Jessica rested her head against his chest, feeling comforted in his strong arms.

Then Tanya waved her purple sweatshirt at them from the lakeside victoriously. "It worked! It worked!" she yelled.

Paul looked at Jessica suspiciously. "I bet you set her up to this."

Jessica gave him a wide-eyed stare, her blue-green eyes innocent. "Who, me?"

Paul looked away angrily. "Women!" he said in disgust. "You can't trust any of them."

"You're just looking for an excuse," Jessica said, a challenge in her eyes.

"An excuse for what?" Paul asked.

"An excuse not to go out with me," Jessica said. "I think you're scared."

Paul pulled her toward him suddenly and gave her a rough kiss.

"Fine, I *will* see you," he stated as he drew back

from her. "But *not* because I like you. Because I want to prove I'm not *afraid* of any woman."

Jessica smiled smugly. It didn't matter *why* Paul agreed to date her—the end result was the same. And for Jessica Wakefield, the ends always justified the means.

"How sweet," she said. Shifting around in her seat, she put her head back against his muscular chest. Jessica closed her eyes contentedly, savoring the feeling of the warm mid-morning sun gently caressing her face as the canoe drifted lazily in the lake.

## Chapter 8

Winston swaggered into the drama cabin on Friday morning, brimming with newfound confidence. He was in charge of lighting for the camp play, and he had promised Joey he would come by to help out. He was wearing red jeans and a T-shirt that said DANGER! HIGH VOLTAGE! on the back. He walked comfortably in his oversize boots now, and his cowboy hat rested low on his forehead.

"Hey, Winston, up here!" Joey yelled from the stage. The drama cabin was almost deserted except for a few people setting up scenery.

Practicing his new macho walk, Winston sauntered slowly up the aisle. He took the four steps leading to the stage two at a time.

Joey whistled when he saw him. "What's this? You trying to drive the girls wild?" he teased.

"You got it, man," Winston said, twirling a piece of grass in his mouth.

"Listen, thanks for coming by," Joey said. "Let me just get you set up in the back." Joey led Winston through a maze of props to the lighting system at the rear of the stage.

Winston's eyes almost popped out of his head when he took in the assortment of wires and cables strewn on the floor. Lightbulbs of almost every size and color were scattered amid the wires. When Winston had volunteered for the job, he had thought his responsibilities would be dimming the lights when the curtain closed. He hadn't realized he was actually supposed to *build* the lighting system.

Joey kicked through the wires and pulled out an extension cord with about sixteen sockets. "The idea is to get everything connected to this one cord. Then we just have to use the remote control to manage the lights on the stage." He held up a black remote-control panel. "See? All you have to do is click."

"Well, the clicking part sounds easy enough," Winston said, holding his head worriedly. "It's the connecting business I'm concerned about."

"Don't worry, it looks more complicated than it is," Joey reassured him. He picked up a red cord off the floor. "All the cords are color coded. Just connect like cords to like cords. Red to red, blue to blue, white to white, and so on."

Winston lifted an eyebrow. He still wasn't convinced that it was easy. "Well, if you hear an explosion, you'll know what happened."

Joey laughed and patted him on the back. "I'm not worried about it," he said. "I've got faith in you."

After Joey walked away, Winston sat down on the

floor in front of the mass of twisted wires and studied the equipment. He felt completely overwhelmed. He was good at chemistry and biology, but practical things were not his forte. *Just take it one step at a time,* he told himself. Taking a deep breath, he began separating the cords and putting them in piles according to category. When that was done, he picked up two red cords, twisting the wires of one and inserting it into the other.

Fifteen minutes later Winston was humming to himself as he worked. He was making progress. Almost all the red cords were attached, and so far he hadn't electrocuted himself. Maybe he wasn't so technically inept after all.

Suddenly he felt someone breathing on his neck.

"I'm dangerous, too," came a low voice behind him. Winston whirled around. It was Lara, and she was looking over his shoulder at his work in progress. His heart raced at the sight of her. She was wearing a burnt orange baby doll dress, and her fiery hair was piled high up on her head. Wispy copper strands framed her delicate face.

Winston coughed and backed away. "Uh, hi, Lara," he said.

"Joey said you're working on the lighting," Lara said, a hand on her hip. "Need an assistant?"

"No, thanks. I think I'm OK," Winston said, trying to keep his voice steady. Just her presence made him nervous.

"What's wrong?" Lara asked with laughing eyes. "You afraid I'm going to light you on fire?"

Winston's face flamed. Flustered, he looked down

quickly and pulled out two cords from the pile. He was so rattled that he didn't pay attention to what he was doing. Lifting the cords in the air, he accidentally touched a section of exposed wiring. A white flash surrounded his finger, and a shock zipped up Winston's arm. Startled, he dropped the cords.

Lara laughed. "You definitely need my help. I'm the stage manager for the plays at my school. I've done this a million times." Lara took a seat next to him and picked up a cord. "I'll do blue. You do red."

Still frazzled, Winston reached for a red cord. Lara was sitting so close to him that he could feel the heat emanating from her body. Winston sighed. Spending time with Lara was *much* more dangerous than electrical wiring.

"So, have you gotten any more letters from Maria?" Lara asked.

Winston nodded, grimacing. "Another 'Hank' letter," he said.

Lara shook her head. "You deserve better than that. Maybe I'll write my own letter to you." She smiled. "Then you'll know what *real* love letters are supposed to sound like."

Winston gulped. Maybe it would have been better if he had gotten electrocuted.

Elizabeth flipped onto her back and stared at the ceiling of the cabin on Friday night. She couldn't sleep. It had been "lights out" for over an hour, and Elizabeth had been tossing and turning since. It was a hot, muggy night. Mosquitoes were biting at her legs, and a fly was droning around her head.

Elizabeth threw back her sheet and slipped out of bed. Fumbling in the dark, she pulled on shorts and a T-shirt and grabbed her flashlight. She decided to go to the boathouse to think. She thought of it as her and Joey's special place.

*It's all for the best,* Elizabeth reassured herself as she made her way through the woods. Now she wouldn't have to lie to Todd. Joey was just a summer fling anyway. When she got back to Sweet Valley, Joey would just fade away to a memory.

But at the moment, all she could think of was Joey. She could see him smiling at her, his green eyes crinkling and his dimple deepening. She could hear him saying her name in that special soft way of his. She could smell the fresh denim of his jean jacket as he held her close to him. And she could taste the salty flavor of his lips as he brought them down on hers. A sudden pain hit her heart as she thought of their stolen kiss in the cave underneath the earth while playing Sardines.

Elizabeth shook her head. *Concentrate on Todd,* she told herself. But even though he had just left, she could barely picture him in her mind.

Elizabeth slipped off her sandals and made her way across the sand. She waded into the lake and walked along the water's edge, following the contours of the lake. No matter how she tried, she couldn't convince herself that it was better this way. She realized that she was fooling herself.

*I've made a mistake. A terrible mistake.* Elizabeth kicked at the sand. *And now there's no way to correct it.*

112

*Or is there?* Elizabeth stood still and gazed out at the moon. Maria was right. The only way out of it at this point was to tell the truth. Standing under the light of the moon, Elizabeth made a firm decision. Her lying had only gotten her into trouble. It was time to come clean to both Joey and Todd. Then maybe she would have a chance with Joey. And Nicole couldn't do anything to hurt her. Elizabeth would tell Todd herself.

Feeling at peace with herself at last, she walked up the beach to the boathouse with a light step. In the solitude of the boathouse, she would figure out how to explain everything to Joey and Todd.

As she approached the boathouse she stopped in her tracks. There were noises coming from inside.

Elizabeth stood still and listened, trying to make out the sounds. Indistinct voices wafted through the air. People were in there. One was female and one was male. A sudden instinctive fear seized her. Nicole's bunk had been empty when Elizabeth had left the cabin. *Is she in there? Who is she with?*

Holding her breath, Elizabeth crept up to the door and listened carefully. Then a shock of recognition jolted her body. The voices belonged to Nicole and Joey, and they were whispering and giggling together. Elizabeth's heart plunged.

Elizabeth stood still, stunned. How could he get involved with Nicole so *fast*? Had the whole thing with Joey been a lie? Did Joey want Nicole after all? Had the two of them been plotting against her all along?

Elizabeth forced herself to calm down. Her imagination was working overtime.

Suddenly everything grew quiet. Her heart sounding a drumroll in her chest, Elizabeth put her ear to the wall. She heard the rustle of clothing and a few murmurs. They were kissing.

Elizabeth yanked her face away, feeling as if her ear had been burned. Her heart crumpling into a million pieces, Elizabeth turned and ran away. Tears blurred her vision as she raced blindly up the shore.

Late that night Jessica lay in bed, fully dressed.

"Meet me at midnight," Paul had said the day before. Now she tingled with excitement. They had a rendezvous planned in the woods next to camp.

Jessica looked at her alarm clock on the side table. It was eleven thirty. Finally. She had been lying awake for hours, staring at the shadows on the ceiling and dreaming about Paul.

Jessica slid silently to the floor and slipped her feet into her tennis shoes. Then she reached under her pillow and felt for her flashlight. The flashlight rolled off the bed and landed on the floor with a clatter. Jessica froze.

"Hmm, mrphh, hmm hmmm?" Lila said, turning over in the bunk. Jessica held her breath, hoping she hadn't woken her. Moments later she heard the sounds of Lila's ladylike snores. Sweeping the flashlight off the floor, she crept out of the cabin and closed the door carefully behind her.

Jessica shone the beam in front of her and headed for the forest. She broke a long branch off a tree to use as a walking stick and entered the dark woods. She felt brave and rebellious, like the heroine in the play. Just like Alexandra, she was risking everything for her one true love. If Lacey caught her, she was sure to send her home. Jessica whacked some shrubbery out of her way with the stick and marched determinedly through the deserted woods.

Fifteen minutes later Jessica's initial excitement had waned. Now she just felt scared. The woods were dark and ominous. The forest seemed to have a life of its own at night. She could see the vegetation moving with invisible insects, and she could hear rodents running by underfoot. Jessica shivered. She wondered if there were bears out here. Or poisonous snakes. Or *wolves*. Suddenly an owl hooted and Jessica jumped.

Taking a deep breath, Jessica picked up her pace. *"Ouch!"* she muttered as she whacked her knee against a big log standing upright in the path. Rubbing her knee, she looked at the piece of wood in horror. What was a freshly cut log doing in the middle of the forest?

The camp legend came back to her, and a chill raced up her spine. What if the woodsman really did haunt the forest? And what if he liked to chop up sixteen-year-old girls and use them for firewood? She knew Lacey probably just made up the story to keep them from sneaking out at night, but still . . .

Jessica breathed a sigh of relief as she caught sight of the fallen tree where she was supposed to meet Paul. She hoped he wouldn't be late.

Practically running through the clearing to the tree, Jessica hopped up on the trunk and waited. She swung her feet in the air casually, trying to pretend she wasn't afraid. Jessica knew it had to be just about midnight. Where was Paul?

Suddenly she saw a shadow moving.

"Paul?" Jessica called out. There was no response. The shadow moved toward her.

"Paul, this isn't funny!" Jessica cried loudly. No response.

Her hair standing on end, Jessica slid quickly off the trunk and began to run. The distinct sound of footsteps followed her. She was terrified. After just a few moments she felt lost. Out of breath, she collapsed against a tree.

Suddenly strong arms circled her waist.

"Aaaah!" Jessica yelled, letting out a bloodcurdling scream. She struggled with all her might against her captor. "Let me go!" she shouted. But her efforts were to no avail. The stranger's arms felt like iron locked around her.

"Jess, I thought you wanted to keep our meeting secret," a soft voice whispered in her ear. It was Paul. Jessica collapsed weakly against him.

Then she turned to face him and pounded on his chest, furious. "If you're trying to prove to me that I am just as scared as you are, it's not a very good way." Jessica was livid. "Scaring a girl in the middle of the night is not funny. It's *stupid*."

Paul caught her fists in his and held them still against his chest. "Jessica, I didn't mean to scare you," he said softly.

Jessica pulled out of his arms. "Then why were you following me?" she asked in indignation. "I saw your shadow the whole time."

"Jess, I swear, the shadow wasn't me," Paul insisted. "You must have been seeing things."

"I know I wasn't seeing things," Jessica insisted. She couldn't figure it out. She knew her mind wasn't playing tricks on her. Something was out there. Feeling spooked, Jessica leaned in close to Paul. He wrapped a comforting arm around her and led her back to the tree.

"Look. I've got a little surprise for you," Paul said, pointing to a spread on the ground. A wicker picnic basket and two wineglasses were laid out on a blanket. A baguette peeked out of the napkin covering the top of the basket. Paul knelt and lifted off the napkin, revealing a bunch of red grapes, Brie cheese, and a jug of sparkling apple cider.

Jessica was touched. "You went to so much trouble," she said softly.

"It was nothing," Paul said, waving a dismissive hand.

"Well, I've certainly built up an appetite from my chase through the woods," Jessica said, sitting down against the tree trunk. "Let's eat."

"OK," Paul agreed, kneeling next to her. "But first, I think you need some comforting." He pulled her to him and kissed her passionately, sending a thrill down her spine. She didn't know if it was the thrill of terror or the excitement of his kiss that was setting her nerve endings on fire.

"That was to make you feel better," Paul said. Then he kissed her again, this time more tenderly. Cupping her chin in one hand, he looked into her eyes and smiled. "And that was to prove I'm not scared."

o　　　o　　　o

Jessica sneaked back into the cabin at two A.M. She was exhausted and exhilarated at the same time. All the girls were sound asleep except Lila. She was lying awake in her bunk, flipping through a fashion magazine with her penlight.

"What are you doing up?" Jessica whispered.

Lila smiled an idiotic lovesick smile. "I couldn't sleep. All I could think of was Beau-re-gard." Jessica rolled her eyes as Lila drew out his name, pronouncing it with a French *r*. She decided she liked Lila better single. She had forgotten how *sappy* Lila could be when she was in love.

Lila's bunk was right next to Jessica's. Not wanting to wake the other girls, Jessica decided to climb over Lila to get to her bed. Holding a finger up to her lips, she stepped up onto Lila's bunk and tried to step over her. But Lila grabbed her ankle midair, and Jessica tumbled onto the bed. The girls stifled giggles.

"And what were you doing out so late, young lady?" Lila asked, putting down her magazine and frowning. "What happened to your boyless summer?"

"I was just in the bathroom," Jessica said.

Lila raised a perfectly arched eyebrow. "For two hours?" she asked.

Jessica nodded solemnly, and the girls burst out in laughter.

Nicole flipped on her side with a loud *hummph* and shot them a dirty look. "Do you mind?" she complained groggily. "Some of us are trying to sleep."

Jessica decided she'd been caught. She was dying to confide in Lila anyway. Half the fun of dating somebody was telling her best friend all about it.

"Come outside," she mouthed to Lila, stepping quietly to the floor and creeping to the door. Lila grabbed the nearest pair of shoes and followed behind in her nightgown.

As she shut the door behind her Lila sat down on the steps to put on her shoes. She had taken Jessica's new hiking boots by mistake. "Ugh, I took your clodhoppers," Lila said, crinkling her nose in distaste. Jamming her feet into the boots, she quickly laced them up.

Lila stood and looked down at her outfit, an expression of horror on her face. Jessica had to laugh at the ridiculous figure Lila made. She was wearing a delicate knee-length white cotton nightgown that contrasted sharply with Jessica's solid brown hiking boots.

"Good thing Bo's not here to see me in this getup," Lila said.

"I thought he liked you for your mind," Jessica teased.

"*And* my fashion sense," Lila said.

Jessica put her hands to her cheeks. "Whatever would Bo's mom say if this fashion faux pas got out?" she teased. "I can just see the headlines now. 'Lila Fowler caught wearing her nightie and boots. All Paris is talking about it. It's a *scandale*.'"

"You're the one whose *life* is a *scandale*," Lila retorted. "Now would you please tell me about mystery man?" Then she held up a hand. "Wait, let me guess."

Jessica shook her head. "You'll never figure it out."

"Just give me three tries," Lila said.

"OK, OK," Jessica said. She pointed to some fallen tree branches in the clearing in the woods. "Let's go sit over there." Jessica flicked on her flashlight and led the way.

Once they were seated, Lila turned a superior face to Jessica. "Actually, I've known who it is all along," she said with a smirk. "I knew there was no way you'd make it through a whole summer without a guy. It's Derek."

Jessica made a face. "What in the world would make you think that?" she asked.

"It makes perfect sense," Lila said. "He's gorgeous, he looks just like Ken, and he's got a crush on you."

"But I don't have a crush on him," Jessica pointed out.

"You don't?" Lila asked.

Jessica shook her head.

"Hmm, that's a problem." Lila thought for a moment. Then she snapped her fingers. "I've got it! It's Joey!"

"Joey!" Jessica exclaimed, looking insulted. "You know Elizabeth is interested in him, even though she tries to deny it. Do you really think I would go after my sister's guy?"

Lila lifted an eyebrow. "Stranger things have happened. *Many* times."

"Humph." Jessica pouted.

"If it's not Derek or Joey, then who else could it be?" Lila wondered aloud. "Justin Siena's got a girlfriend at home, Winston Egbert's become a cowboy, Buford and Johansen aren't even a consideration."

Lila shrugged. "There simply aren't any guys in this camp you would be interested in."

Jessica smiled.

"Aha!" Lila said. "He's not in the camp." She shook her head. "Of course. Why didn't I think of it before? It's Paul, Tanya's older brother—the one who kept asking about you all weekend."

Jessica grinned. "Third time's the charm," she said.

"I can't believe it!" Lila exclaimed. She gave Jessica a stern look. "How could you keep something so big from me? How in the world have you been seeing him? Have you been sneaking out at night?" Lila crossed her arms over her chest. "Tell me *everything*."

Jessica was only too happy to oblige. She recounted the whole affair in great detail, from her first meeting with Paul at the girls' cabin to their last meeting in the woods. "I don't think anything would have happened if I hadn't kidnapped him," Jessica finished.

"Jessica Wakefield, sometimes you are just too much," Lila said.

"Li, don't tell anyone, OK?" Jessica said. "Especially Elizabeth."

"Of course not," Lila responded. "She would totally freak out."

"Oh, and one more thing," Jessica added. "Can you cover for me if I need you to?"

"You got it, Jess," Lila said with a smile. "After all, what are friends for?"

# Chapter 9

"Nicole, Nicole, wake up!" Maria said, shaking her friend on Saturday morning at the girls' cabin.

Elizabeth scowled as she laced up her tennis shoes, feeling betrayed by Maria. All the JCs were up and dressed except Nicole. The day's activities included a treasure hunt for all the campers and a campfire that evening. Elizabeth had been hoping that Nicole would sleep through all her duties and get thrown out of camp.

"Mmm," Nicole murmured luxuriously. She smiled contentedly and turned on her side, wrapping the sheet around her body.

Maria shook her again. "Nicole, get up! You're going to be late for breakfast."

Nicole opened her eyes and squinted at Maria. "Is it morning already?" she asked in a groggy voice. "I feel like I just went to bed."

"Yes, it is. In fact, it's been morning for quite a

while," Maria said. "You better get moving. You've got fifteen minutes before breakfast."

Nicole sat up in bed and ran her fingers through her disheveled hair. She was wearing an oversize white T-shirt that said CAMP ECHO MOUNTAIN DRAMA CLUB on it. Two thespian masks were embossed on the breast pocket.

With a start, Elizabeth recognized the T-shirt. It was Joey's. It was the same shirt that he'd been wearing the night of the Sardine game. He must have given it to Nicole last night. Elizabeth's stomach turned at the thought.

Nicole stretched and yawned lazily. "I was just having the most *scrumptious* dream," she said.

"Well, tell us all about it while you get dressed," Maria said, shooing her off the bed.

Nicole swung her two long, tanned legs over the side of her bed. "It was about me and Joey," she said. "We were on this desert island, just the two of us. We were staying in a tent on the beach. Then we took a midnight swim in the ocean—" Her eyes glazed over and her voice faded away.

Jessica laughed. She was sitting on her bunk, brushing her hair. "Keep dreaming, Nicole."

Nicole hopped out of bed and grabbed a pair of rumpled jeans that were hanging over her trunk. "It's not a dream," she said lightly, pulling on the jeans.

Jessica lifted an eyebrow. "What do you mean, it's not a dream?" she asked.

"You really *were* on a desert island with Joey?" Lila added, reaching her hands behind her head to fasten a necklace.

123

"Well, not a desert island," Nicole said. "The beach on the lake."

"Wait a minute, are you saying you got together with Joey?" Angela asked, her deep brown eyes sparkling with excitement. Elizabeth rolled her eyes. At first she had thought she and Angela could become friends. Angela was sweet and good-natured and shared Elizabeth's passion for books. But then Nicole had gotten Angela on her side. Elizabeth and Angela barely spoke to each other now.

Nicole picked up a comb off her bureau and ran it through her hair. "Yep, last night," she said casually.

"But you were in the cabin last night," Angela said, looking confused. "You went to bed with the rest of us."

Nicole smiled. "I wasn't in the cabin for long."

"You snuck out last night?" Angela asked.

Nicole nodded. She picked up her backpack and slung it over her right shoulder. "So, are you guys ready?" she asked.

"Oh, no, you don't," Angela protested, blocking the door. "We want details."

"Well . . . if you really want to know . . . ," Nicole began, looking around her. Everybody nodded.

Elizabeth snorted with disgust. Nicole's little game was making her sick. Elizabeth knew it would be better to leave before she heard any more, but her curiosity overcame her. Even though it was painful, she wanted to know what happened last night between Joey and Nicole.

Nicole sauntered down the aisle. "Let's see. Joey and I met late last night at a secret spot in the woods.

124

It was *so* romantic. You can tell he's an older guy." Nicole perched on the edge of a bunk, a dreamy look on her face. "First we had a picnic by candlelight in the woods. Then we took a walk along the lake in the moonlight. And just a little after midnight we took a swim in the lake."

Elizabeth sat down hard on her bunk, feeling as though she'd been physically assaulted. Each word was like a blow to her heart.

"Nicole! You're torturing us!" Angela declared. "Get to the good part."

"And then we went to the boathouse to talk," Nicole said. Then she smiled. "But we didn't get a lot of talking done. We were sitting on one of those overturned canoes when Joey pulled me in his arms and kissed me. I've never met anyone who kisses like that. . . ."

Angela was right. Nicole was torturing her. Elizabeth couldn't stand to hear one more word. She grabbed her bag off her bed and slipped quietly out of the cabin.


"Hey, Jess, want a s'more?" Derek asked.

"Sure," she said, taking the chocolate-and-marshmallow graham cracker sandwich from him.

It was Saturday night and Jessica was sitting with all the counselors around a crackling campfire. They were singing camp songs and cooking marshmallows. The campers had all gone to bed an hour ago.

Joey picked up his guitar and started strumming on it. "And the seasons, they go round and round," he sang in a low voice. "And the painted ponies go up and down. We're captured on a carousel of time. . . ." As he sang the refrain of the popular song the other counselors joined in.

Jessica took a bite into the sweet concoction, feeling a pang of longing for Paul. She usually found camp songs corny, but the pretty tune was making her feel sentimental. The mood of the group was mellow and romantic. It seemed like everybody was paired up. Lila and Bo were sitting close together. Angela and Justin were holding hands. Nicole was gazing at Joey, starstruck, as he played. Only Elizabeth was missing. She probably couldn't handle seeing Nicole and Joey together. Jessica didn't blame her. It was nauseating watching that girl sinking her claws into Joey.

"Looks like the scene has gotten pretty hot and heavy here," Derek said, taking a seat next to her.

Jessica smiled. "Good thing we're here to keep it cool, huh?"

Derek clutched at his heart as if a dagger had been thrust in it. "You are one tough lady, Jessica Wakefield," he said. Gathering a handful of twigs from the ground, he threw it into the fire. The fire flamed bright orange and yellow.

Derek's attention only made her feel more lonely. Jessica had no interest in talking to him. She was itching to see Paul. She stared into the flickering flames, wishing that Paul were sitting beside her. She longed to snuggle in his arms by the warmth of the fire. But that wasn't possible. If Jessica wanted to see him, she would have to go to him.

It was a tempting thought. She could borrow

Lacey's car again and sneak out. Lacey would be sleeping by now, and the campfire was set up far away from the main lodge. But a little voice in her head stopped her. It was too risky. Somebody might see her go. She should wait until lights-out.

The fire crackled in the dark night. Bo pulled Lila closer to him, and Angela and Justin got up to take a walk, hand in hand. Jessica decided she couldn't wait any longer. She stood up impetuously. She had to see Paul. And she had to see him now.

Jessica walked around the campfire to Lila and Bo. "Lila," she said. "I need to talk to you." She took her arm and pulled her away from the fire.

"Jess!" Lila complained, yanking her arm away and rubbing it. "Bo and I were having a moment."

"Don't worry, you'll have time for plenty more of them," Jessica said. Then she lowered her voice to a whisper. "Listen, you've got to cover for me. I'm going to go see Paul at the restaurant."

"How are you going to get there?" Lila asked.

"I'm going to take a ride in Lacey's truck," Jessica explained.

Lila looked at her as if she were stark raving mad. "Jessica, have you lost your mind?"

Jessica shrugged. "It's no big deal. Lacey's sleeping already."

"But what if she wakes up? What if she comes to the campfire?" Lila asked worriedly.

"Then you've got to make up some story. Tell her I'm with Liz, having an identity crisis or something," Jessica said.

"She'll never believe me," Lila said.

127

Jessica patted her on the shoulder. "Don't worry. It probably won't happen. And if it does, you'll think of something." She turned to go. "See you tomorrow. And don't wait up!"

"Jessica, this is pushing the limits of friendship too far!" Lila protested.

But Jessica was already walking away. "Thanks, Lila!" she called. "I owe you one."

"I thought I'd find you here!" Maria said on Saturday evening. Elizabeth was sitting alone on the dock, swinging her legs in the water.

"Oh, hi, Maria," Elizabeth said. Usually just the sight of Maria caused Elizabeth's spirits to brighten, but today she was barely able to summon the energy to smile at her friend.

Maria sat down next to her and put an arm around her shoulders. "You all right?" she asked.

"Not really," Elizabeth said. She didn't know when she'd felt so glum. It had been bad enough breaking up with Joey in the cafeteria, but it was devastating to see him with Nicole.

"Joey and Nicole are getting to you, huh?" Maria said sympathetically.

Elizabeth nodded. She was glad Maria had found her. She needed to confide in somebody. "I just can't handle seeing Nicole and Joey together."

"Yeah, it's hard enough breaking up with someone, but it's always worse seeing them with someone else," Maria said.

"That's exactly it," Elizabeth said. "I just can't believe Joey could get over me so fast."

"Well, maybe he's just hurt," Maria suggested. "Sometimes it's good to jump into a new relationship to get over the pain of an old one."

"But how could Joey get involved with Nicole after all he knows about her?" Elizabeth persisted. "That girl does not have one redeeming characteristic."

"Well, actually she does have a lot of good qualities," Maria said diplomatically. "She's pretty in a natural-looking way, and she has a really original style. And she's a great water-skier on top of it."

"Maria, how can you say that?" Elizabeth protested. "It doesn't matter what Nicole looks like or what she does. What matters is the kind of person she is. And that girl is a manipulative, cunning little snake."

"I think you're being too hard on her," Maria said. "After all, everybody makes mistakes."

Elizabeth's mouth dropped open. "Mistakes! You call stealing my play a mistake? And claiming it as her own a mistake? And stealing Joey a mistake?"

"I'm not condoning Nicole's actions," Maria said. "I'm just trying to understand them."

Elizabeth fell silent. Maybe she should listen to what her friend had to say. Maria had a sixth sense about people that rarely fell short of the mark.

"Maybe she felt justified in blackmailing you on some level," Maria surmised. "Maybe she felt like she deserved Joey. After all, you do have a boyfriend."

Elizabeth opened her mouth to defend herself, but then she shut it.

"I mean, it's not really fair of you to want both

Todd and Joey at the same time," Maria pointed out. "You can't blame Joey for dating someone else, and you can't expect Nicole to keep away from him just because you have a crush on him."

Elizabeth stared out at the water, feeling put in her place. Maria was right. Elizabeth wanted to have her cake and eat it, too. She had tried to juggle two guys at the same time, and now she was paying the price. She was getting exactly what she deserved—misery.

Jessica cruised along the two-lane highway into town, feeling exhilarated. She rolled down the window and hummed to herself as the wind whipped through her hair.

Her escape had gone off without a hitch. Nobody had seen her go, and Lacey hadn't woken up. Jessica had slipped in the door of Lacey's house and had silently lifted the keys to the Bronco from a hook in the kitchen. Lacey kept the truck parked on an incline behind the main lodge. Jessica had climbed in and shifted into neutral, and the truck had slid soundlessly down the hill. Now she was home free.

Jessica saw the lights of Paul's family's diner up ahead and cut her speed. It was called Mattie's and had a blinking red neon sign in front. The parking lot was jammed with cars.

Jessica backed up carefully into a free spot and hopped out of the truck. Her heart beating with excitement, she made her way across the lot and threaded her way through the crowd at the door. She didn't see Paul anywhere.

"Would you like a table?" asked the host, looking down at the list in his hand as she walked in.

"No, thanks," Jessica said. "They're expecting me in back."

Acting as if she knew what she was doing, Jessica marched breezily into the kitchen. A man in a chef's hat and long white apron was standing at the counter, dicing vegetables. His worn face was red and moist from the heat in the kitchen.

Jessica walked past the counter and turned the corner. Then she caught sight of Paul from the back. He was flipping hamburgers on the grill.

"Four well done and two medium rare!" yelled the cook from the kitchen.

"Gotcha, chief!" Paul yelled back.

"Two rare to go," Jessica said from behind his back.

At the sound of her voice Paul wheeled around, spatula in hand. "Jessica!" he exclaimed. With his free arm he pulled her to him and gave her a big kiss. "What are you doing here?"

"I was just kind of hungry, so I thought I'd stop by," Jessica said with a smile.

"Hungry for a burger?" Paul asked teasingly.

Jessica shook her head. "Hungry for you," she said.

"Well, I'm hungry for you, too, but unfortunately I can't get off," Paul said. "We're always really busy Saturday night, and I told my parents I'd help out."

Jessica's face fell. She couldn't have come all this way for nothing. "Can't you just take a quick break?"

"Sorry," Paul said, looking apologetic. "This is our

busiest time. We've got the late-night crowd now. Things will wind down in about an hour."

"Well, then, how about if I help out, too?" Jessica offered.

Paul looked at her in surprise. "I thought sophisticated girls like you were afraid to get their hands dirty."

"For your information, I've been a waitress before," Jessica returned. "And *I'm* not afraid of anything!" She gave him a pointed look.

"Touché!" Paul said, laughing.

Jessica grabbed a long white apron from the counter and threw it over her head. She tied it securely in the back and twisted her hair into a knot on her head. Then she marched over to the grill and picked up a spatula.

"Two medium rare!" yelled the cook, sticking his head around the corner.

"Coming up!" Jessica returned. She picked up two meat patties and threw them on the grill.

The cook did a double take. "What's this?" he asked.

Paul smiled. "We've got some extra help tonight," he explained.

"At last," the cook said. "Now maybe the food will go out in time." He winked at Jessica and disappeared around the corner.

Paul slung an arm over her shoulders as she flipped the burgers. "You never cease to surprise me," he said.

An hour and a half later Jessica fell exhausted into a booth. She was drenched in perspiration and her face was flushed pink. Jessica lifted up her arms, airing out her blouse. She felt like she had been swimming in her blouse and jeans.

Not only was she uncomfortable, but she was in pain. Her arms and shoulders were aching from cooking and cleaning. She and Paul had worked at the grill nonstop for an hour straight. Then they had closed down the restaurant and scrubbed the whole place.

"I never want to see another hamburger again," Jessica announced.

"Now you know what it's like working in the back," Paul said with a smile, sliding in next to her in the booth.

Jessica slipped out of her shoes and wiggled her toes. "I think I'd rather be on the ordering side of the restaurant business." Paul put his hands on her shoulders, and she leaned back in his arms.

"Hey, Jess, you know what?" Paul said in her ear. "I decided I kind of like you—a little."

Jessica smiled at him. "I like you, too. But only a little."

Paul pulled her close and kissed her.

Then Jessica looked at the wooden clock on the wall. "Omigosh, I've gotta go! It's almost two in the morning." She jumped up and slipped into her shoes.

Paul hurried ahead of her and held open the door of the diner. "After you, madam," he said.

Jessica shivered as the cool air hit her wet clothes. The parking lot was deserted now, and the night was pitch-black.

Paul wrapped an arm around her shoulders and

walked her across the lot. "Promise to drive safely?" he asked.

"Of course, you know me!" Jessica said in a flippant tone.

"I think I'm beginning to," Paul said. "And that's what I'm worried about."

When they reached the Ford Bronco, Paul pulled opened the front door and Jessica climbed into the driver's seat. "When will I see you again?" he asked.

"I'll sneak out again in two days," Jessica promised.

Paul leaned in and gave her a kiss. "I'll be waiting," he said.

Jessica's heart was soaring as she drove back to camp on the empty highway. Paul had been completely different this time. The first time she had visited him, he had been as icy as a glacier. But this time Paul had been completely receptive to her. He was really beginning to open up. Two days seemed like an eternity.

But as she approached the campgrounds, she began to feel nervous. Maybe Lila was right. Maybe she was crazy to take such a risk. What if Lacey had woken up? What if she had noticed that her keys were missing? Or that her car was gone?

Jessica chewed on her lower lip as she exited the highway. Her parents would kill her if they found out she had driven to town alone at this hour. She could just hear Lacey calling them to report her. "Jessica sneaked out of camp in the middle of the night in a stolen vehicle—mine." Her parents would ground her for an entire year. Maybe for the rest of high school.

Instead of driving directly to the main lodge, Jessica followed the dirt road around the lake. At the top of the hill she cut the engine and turned off the lights. Shifting into neutral, she let the car slide down the incline. As she coasted past the main lodge she pressed her foot slowly onto the brake. The car came to a quiet halt.

Her heart pounding, Jessica scrambled out of the car and silently shut the door. She quickly looked around the deserted clearing, half expecting to see Lacey standing by the side of the road with Jessica's parents by her side. But nobody was there. Relief coursed through her veins.

Then a light went on in Lacey's cabin.

Jessica ducked behind a tree, her heart pounding like a jackhammer. She could see the front door of Lacey's cabin swing open. Lacey marched out in her robe, carrying a huge flashlight.

"Who's there?" Lacey called, shining the light through the trees. "What's going on?"

Jessica stood perfectly still as Lacey scoured the area. The owner crunched through the woods around the cabin, circling the house. Then she headed for the main lodge. "Is anybody there?" she called, opening the door. She disappeared inside for a few minutes.

Jessica resisted the temptation to run away. If Lacey heard the sound of her footsteps, she would be sure to follow her.

A moment later Lacey reappeared. "I know you're

out there," she yelled, "so you might as well give yourself up!"

Jessica held her breath as Lacey stopped directly in front of the tree she was hiding behind. Lacey shone the light left and right, as if she could sense Jessica's presence.

Finally the owner gave up. Shrugging, she went back into the house, letting the screen door swing shut behind her.

Jessica exhaled slowly, her whole body trembling in relief. Tiptoeing out of her hiding place, she sneaked carefully around the main lodge. Then she dashed across the clearing into the security of the dark woods.

*That was a close call,* Jessica thought as she hurried through the trees. *Too close. I'll have to be a lot more careful next time.*

# Chapter 10

"Mmm, nothing better than a Sunday in the sun," Lila murmured, lying flat on her back on the blanket and closing her eyes.

"Finally a day of freedom," Jessica agreed, enjoying the feel of the hot sun beating down on her body.

Jessica and Lila were sunbathing on Sunday afternoon on the small strip of empty sand between the girls' cabins and the center of camp. This Sunday the junior counselors had the day off, and Jessica and Lila decided to spend it together.

Lila turned a sandy face to Jessica. "Jess, the next time you decide to sneak out, do you think you can wait until everybody's in bed? I was so worried that Lacey was going to show up that I was a nervous wreck the whole evening. I kept looking around so much that Bo asked me if I had a twitch in my neck."

Jessica sat up and smoothed suntan lotion on her

legs. "Sorry, Li, it won't happen again. I just couldn't wait any longer last night."

Lila shook her head. "And you said *I* was whipped." She reached for her sunglasses and put them on. "Well, I hope it was worth it."

"It was definitely worth it," Jessica confirmed.

"Why, what did you two do?" Lila asked.

Jessica pulled a bottle of mineral water out of her straw beach bag and took a big gulp. "We grilled hamburgers in the kitchen of the restaurant," she said dreamily. "It was *so* romantic."

Lila took off her sunglasses and stared at her, appalled. "You call that romantic?"

Jessica nodded. "I call that heaven."

Lila shook her head and closed her eyes again. "You have definitely gone off your rocker."

Suddenly the loudspeaker system crackled.

"Uh-oh, I hear a voice from above," Lila muttered.

Lacey's voice boomed across the camp. "Attention, all counselors! Attention, all counselors! There will be an important meeting in the main lodge in fifteen minutes. Attendance is mandatory."

Lila moaned. "Our one day off and Lacey calls a meeting."

Jessica flipped on her stomach and rested her head on her hands. "Let's not go. Elizabeth can brief us later."

But Lila was throwing on her clothes. She held out a hand to Jessica and pulled her up. "Jessica Wakefield, the meeting is *mandatory*. You're obviously trying to get yourself kicked out of camp, and

138

I'm not about to let you abandon me here. Now c'mon."

"OK, OK," Jessica said, getting up reluctantly and gathering her stuff. "Lila, you're such a worrywart."

Fifteen minutes later all the counselors were clustered in the auditorium of the main lodge. Jessica and Lila were sitting in the back row, next to Aaron and Winston.

"Thank you for coming on such short notice," Lacey said from the podium. "I know this is the junior counselors' day off, so I'll be brief."

"Lacey doesn't know the meaning of the word *brief*," Winston whispered.

"Are we all here?" Lacey asked, pushing her horn-rimmed spectacles to the end of her nose and peering through them. She went through roll call, calling out the names of the six junior counselors and six senior counselors.

Aaron leaned over to the others and whispered, "Are we at boot camp?"

"Operation Cavannah in action," Winston said, saluting them. "Sergeant Winston Egbert reporting for duty at oh–eleven hundred hours."

Jessica and Lila giggled.

Lacey shot them an annoyed look. "Ahem!" she said. "I have reason to believe that some of the JCs aren't acting in accordance with the camp rules. Therefore I would like to review those regulations quickly."

Winston groaned. "I feel like I'm in kindergarten."

"I have a copy of the official camp guidelines with

me," Lacey said, holding up a pamphlet. "You all received this in the mail, but in case you've forgotten what it says, I'll just refresh your memories." Lacey pursed her lips and squinted at the page. "JCs are not allowed to keep mixed company in cabins, to have late-night parties, to partake of alcohol or illegal substances, or to sneak across the lake after dark"—she paused and looked directly out into the auditorium— "or into town."

Jessica fidgeted uncomfortably. She felt like Lacey was talking directly to her.

"I would like to remind you that serious infringements of the camp rules will result in expulsion from the premises," Lacey continued.

Then she fixed a steely eye on Jessica. "You should all consider yourselves warned."

"Horseback riding is taking this whole cowboy thing too far," Winston protested as he and Aaron trekked through the woods on Sunday afternoon. They were heading to the camp stables for Winston's first riding lesson. The stables were located in a big manor north of the camp.

Winston was terrified. He had a hard enough time keeping on his feet on solid ground. He had no interest in trying to stay upright on the back of a horse.

"Winston, how can you expect to be a cowboy if you can't ride a horse?" Aaron asked. The sun glared down between the trees, and Aaron pulled his baseball cap lower over his forehead.

"Easily," Winston said. "I'm a modern cowboy. Modern cowboys wear boots and ride in cars. It's time to bring the whole cowboy generation into the nineties."

"Well, you can explain all that to the stable owner," Aaron said. "Maybe he'll close down the whole operation."

The forest opened up into a clearing, and a beautiful pasture met their eyes. A stately white manor stood up on a hill, and the stables were below it. The plantation was surrounded by lush greenery and rolling hills. A few horses grazed in the open meadow.

"This is the perfect spot for horseback riding," Aaron said enthusiastically.

"That's easy for you to say," Winston replied. "You're not the one who has to ride on the back of one of those animals."

Winston and Aaron walked across the meadow and entered the stables. Some senior counselors were giving a riding lesson to a few small campers in a pen. The kids were sitting on the backs of ponies, and the counselors were leading the horses by the reins.

Suddenly Winston felt butterflies flitting around in his stomach. "Aaron, I can't do this," he whispered.

"Of course you can," Aaron reassured him. "Look, even those little kids are riding."

"That's because they're too young to recognize the risks," Winston said. "They don't realize they can fall off and break their legs—or their *necks*!"

"Let's go talk to the stable owner," Aaron said, leading him to the office.

"Aaron, didn't you hear me?" Winston asked, following.

Aaron's response was to cup his hand around his ear. "I'm sorry, did you say something?"

Winston shook his head.

"Can I help you boys?" asked a man behind a desk. "My name's Lewis, but everybody calls me Sky, after my eyes. I'm the ranch hand here." Sky was a tough-looking man with a worn brown face and an easy grin. His eyes really were the color of the sky—a startling pale blue against his tanned skin.

"Hi, Sky. I'm Aaron and this is Winston," Aaron said, holding out a hand. Winston managed a half wave. "Winston would like to take a riding lesson. Do you have a horse available for the afternoon?"

"Sure we do!" Sky said cheerily. He looked Winston over. "I think I've got the perfect horse for a tough guy like you. Just wait outside and I'll be right out."

"Oh, boy," Winston said with fake excitement as they walked outside.

A few minutes later Sky stepped out of stables, leading a beautiful horse by the reins. She was a big black mare with imposing hindquarters and a sleek black tail.

Suddenly the horse whinnied, lifting her front hooves in the air.

At the sight of the rearing creature Winston's eyes almost popped out of his head. "You want me to ride that animal?" he squeaked.

"Don't worry, Silkwood is extremely gentle," Sky reassured him. "Even five-year-olds can ride her." He pulled a sugar cube out of his pocket and fed it to her. The horse bared a set of big white teeth as she nibbled on the sugar.

Winston bit his lip, staring up at the saddle high above him on Silkwood's back. "How am I supposed to get up there?"

"Just put one foot in the stirrup and swing your leg over," Sky said.

"C'mon, Winston, you can do it," Aaron encouraged him.

Winston pulled his cowboy hat low over his forehead and took a deep breath. Summoning his courage, he put a foot in the stirrup and threw his other leg over the horse's back. Falling forward, he pulled himself awkwardly up into a sitting position.

Before he was settled in the saddle, Silkwood took off at a slow trot.

"Yowsee!" Winston yelled, grabbing onto the reins. Silkwood took that as a signal to increase her speed and began to gallop across the field.

Winston clutched the saddle horn and flattened himself against the horse's body. He could feel the air whipping through his hair and the trees whirring by him in a blur. As the horse leaped through the pasture Winston bounced up and down. He felt like he was on a roller coaster gone out of control. Whimpering, he held on for dear life.

Suddenly he felt his grip loosening. "Hce-llp!" he yelled as the momentum swept him out of the saddle. He slid off the sleek horse's side and tumbled to the ground. His cowboy hat fell off and rolled to a stop.

"Well done!" Aaron called from across the field. He ran across the meadow to join him.

When Aaron reached Winston, he asked, "You OK?"

Winston pulled himself up to a sitting position and carefully lifted his arms and legs in the air. "I don't think anything's hurt—except my dignity," he replied.

Aaron dusted off the hat and patted it back down on Winston's head. Silkwood nosed him gently.

"Up you go," Aaron said, helping him back up on the horse.

Winston moaned. It was going to be a long day.


"OK, guys, let's block just one more scene and then we'll call it quits for the night," Joey said on Sunday evening at the drama cabin.

Joey was sitting on the stage with Jessica and Derek. He had called play rehearsal only for the lead actors. He wanted to run through the scenes that featured just the two of them.

Jessica leaned back against a prop on the stage and curled her knees up to her chest. She was glad they were almost finished. They had already blocked four scenes, and Jessica was feeling a little tired. Her late night out and her day in the sun were beginning to catch up with her.

"Now, I want you both to close your eyes and try to picture the scene," Joey instructed. Jessica did as she was told, letting Joey's voice take her back in time to the world of Alexandra and the woodsman.

"This is your final scene," Joey said in a lulling voice. "You're out in the woods together, and you're all alone. There's nothing to eat, so you've been gathering berries. As you meet front center, you give each other a meaningful look and then drop a handful of berries into each other's mouths. You kiss to seal your fate, and then you hold hands and move slowly backward, fading away into the mists of time. The stage goes black. All we hear are the sounds of chopping wood."

Jessica felt herself drifting into her part. The scene stood out vividly in her mind.

"Great!" Derek enthused. "This is my favorite scene."

Derek's voice brought Jessica back to the present with a start.

"Let's practice the kissing part," Derek suggested.

Jessica made a face. "Maybe we should practice the disappearing part."

Joey held up a hand, looking amused. "OK, you two, that's not important for now. Today we're not acting out the scenes. We're just blocking them."

Jessica breathed a sigh of relief. It was bad enough that she was going to have to kiss Derek onstage. The last thing she wanted to do was practice it over and over again.

"Now, I just want to do a run-through without lines," Joey said. "When the scene opens, you two are apart. You're trampling through the forest, looking for berries. Jessica, you're at stage right. Derek, you're at stage left."

Jessica stood up and took her position at the far corner of the stage. Closing her eyes, she tried to get back into the scene.

Suddenly the drama cabin door opened and a shaft of light shone into the room. Jessica's eyes flew open. It was Lacey, and she was marching up the aisle, looking sterner than usual. "Joey, do you mind if I borrow one of your actors for a moment?" she asked.

Jessica's heart plunged. She knew which actor Lacey wanted to see.

"Sure, no problem," Joey said.

"Jessica, do you mind coming with me?" Lacey asked. "I think we need to have a little talk."

Jessica nodded and climbed down the stairs. She bit her lip as she followed Lacey down the aisle. Obviously Lacey knew about last night's incident. *Is she going to kick me out?* Jessica wondered. *Does she have proof? How does she know it was me?*

Jessica's mind raced. She had to come up with an explanation. Maybe she could say there had been an emergency at the restaurant and that Paul needed some supplies. Jessica could explain that she hadn't wanted to wake Lacey and that she knew Lacey would understand. *What kind of emergency?* Jessica wondered. Maybe a small kitchen fire. That was a good idea. Maybe Paul needed fire extinguishers from the main lodge.

Or maybe she could deny it altogether. Lacey couldn't have actual proof. But then, she probably didn't need proof to kick her out. After all, Lacey was the owner of the camp.

Then again, she could just say it was Elizabeth who had sneaked out with the car. Lacey couldn't stand Elizabeth anyway. But then Elizabeth would get kicked out of camp, and she would never speak to Jessica again. The fire was the best option, Jessica decided.

146

"Have a seat, Jessica," Lacey said, leading her to the back row of the auditorium.

Jessica smiled brightly as she settled into a chair. "Did you have something you wanted to talk to me about?" she asked.

"Yes, I did," Lacey said, her face grave. "Jessica, I'm very disappointed in you. I thought you were one of our most responsible counselors, and I trusted you."

"But you see, there was this fire—," Jessica interrupted, launching into her story.

Lacey held up a hand. "I don't want any excuses, and I don't want to hear any stories," she warned.

Jessica shut her mouth.

"I'm not a dumb old lady, Jessica," Lacey said. "I know everything that goes on in my camp." She fixed Jessica with a hard gaze. *"Everything."*

Jessica blanched. She could tell that Lacey wouldn't buy any of her stories. Swallowing hard, she steeled herself for her punishment.

"Because you've been a stellar counselor—up to now—I'm going to give you one more chance," Lacey said.

Jessica nodded, trying not to let her relief show.

"But I want to give you a special warning," Lacey said. Her dark blue eyes glittered as she spoke. "If you pull one more stunt, you're going to be out of this camp faster than you can say 'Camp Echo Mountain.'"

Jessica gulped.

"Have I made myself understood?" Lacey asked.

Jessica nodded and shrank farther down in her seat.

# Chapter 11

Monday morning after breakfast Jessica ran out of the lodge before any of the Wannabees could follow her. She had to get word to Paul that she couldn't come see him this evening. If she hurried, she could catch the mailman when he came to deliver the morning mail.

Rushing across the clearing, Jessica entered the forest and hid herself underneath the low fronds of a weeping willow. Looking around to make sure no one was watching, she pulled out a writing pad from her backpack. Then she felt along the bottom of the bag for a pen. She pulled out a stick of lipstick, then a pair of sunglasses. Frustrated, she dumped the entire contents of her bag on the ground. An assortment of various odds and ends came tumbling out, including a variety of cosmetics, a hairbrush, some writing utensils, a perfume bottle, and a set of keys. Jessica pounced on a ballpoint pen.

Jessica leaned back against the tree and chewed on the end of the pen, trying to decide what to say. She had to make the note somewhat cryptic in case it was intercepted. She didn't want any written proof of her misadventures on Saturday night. But then, she didn't want Paul to think she was blowing him off. He was obviously very sensitive about the issue.

Then she got an idea. She would invite Paul to the play. That way he would know she still wanted to see him. He would understand that something had come up. She was sure he would be able to read between the lines.

Feeling inspired, Jessica rested the pad on her knees and wrote quickly.

*Dear Paul,*
    *I will miss you tonight. I wanted to write to invite you to the play on Wednesday night—Lakeside Love—at eight in the drama cabin. Tanya has a role, so there's no reason you shouldn't be able to attend. Please get word to me that you're coming.*
    *I'm counting the hours until I see you.*

                    *Love,*
                    *Jessica*

Jessica folded up the note and stuffed it in an envelope. Turning the envelope over, she sealed it and added a spray of perfume. Then she scribbled the address of the restaurant on the cover.

Jessica quickly cleaned up the mess on the ground, throwing her belongings back in the bag.

Tucking the letter in the outside pocket, she swung the bag over her shoulder and hurried back to the lodge.

Jessica smiled to herself as she walked in the main doors of the lodge, feeling satisfied with her letter. She tried to picture the look on Paul's face when he read it. He would be disappointed that she wasn't coming, but he would be happy to get word from her. Lila was right. She really *was* having an epistolary romance.

Jessica hurried down the hall and turned into the mail room. Then her face fell when she saw that the boxes had already been stuffed. She must have just missed the mailman.

Then through the window she caught sight of the blue mail truck. Jessica dashed down the hall. She ran out the door just as the truck was pulling away.

"Wait, wait!" Jessica called, chasing after the mailman. He picked up speed as he went down the incline. Jessica flew down the street after him, waving her hand in the air.

At the end of the street the driver caught sight of her in the rearview window and pulled to a stop.

Panting, Jessica jogged up to the window. "Thanks so much for stopping," she said. "I've got an urgent letter that needs to be delivered today." She unzipped her bag and pulled out the letter.

"Two-oh-one North Mountain Road," said the postman, reading the address aloud.

"It's a restaurant in town," Jessica explained.

"Well, they're not going to get that letter today," the man said in a lazy voice. "All mail goes to Helena, the capital of Montana, and is sent out from there. I'd say this letter will take about two to three days."

"Oh, no!" Jessica cried. "But it's just in town, about an hour away from here. Can't you just drop it off on your way out?"

The postman raised an eyebrow. "This isn't a personal delivery service, miss. This is the U.S. Postal Service."

"Can't you please make an exception?" Jessica begged, turning imploring eyes on him. "This is an emergency situation. It's *crucial* that the letter get there this afternoon."

"All right, all right," the postman grumbled, taking it from her hand. "But don't make a habit out of this." He looked at her sternly. "And don't tell anyone I'm doing this for you."

"You got it," Jessica said, her blue-green eyes twinkling. "It's our secret."

"OK, guys, let's run through the mess hall food fight scene," Joey said on Monday afternoon at the drama cabin. "All extras in the cafeteria scene report to the office. Maria will supply you with props."

Elizabeth nudged Maria. "You better get up there. Duty calls." She and Maria were sitting in the back row of the auditorium, watching the play rehearsal. Jessica and most of the kids were in the auditorium. Winston was manning the curtain, and Lara was working the lights with the remote control.

"Oh, you're right," Maria said, jumping up.

"Yeah!" yelled a little girl, running up the stairs.

"Food fight!" an older boy yelled. The kids whistled

and cheered as they clambered onto the stage.

Maria laughed and leaned down to Elizabeth. "You'll love this. The food fight is their favorite scene."

Elizabeth nodded and tried to smile back, but she felt herself grimacing.

"Hey, you OK?" Maria asked, looking concerned.

"Yes, yes, of course," Elizabeth said, shooing Maria away. "Now get up there and do your job."

Maria didn't look convinced. "I'll catch you later," she said. Then she ran up the aisle and hopped up on the stage, disappearing into a sea of screaming children.

Maria had suggested that getting involved with the play might help Elizabeth get her mind off her romantic confusion. Elizabeth had agreed. But now she realized that she had just come to be close to Joey. Watching him was almost more painful than not seeing him at all.

While Maria got the kids set up in back, Joey directed Jessica. "Now, Jess, in the middle of bedlam you appear and walk serenely through the room. The woodsman has been banished from the camp, and you're all alone. The point of this scene is contrast. You are immune to the chaos around you." Jessica nodded.

"As you reach center stage, you make your crucial decision," Joey continued. "The spotlight shines on you for your soliloquy. 'In the flicker of an instant, my fate will be sealed. Why should someone so young be forced to grow up so quickly?'"

But as Joey recited the lines, he didn't look at Jessica at all. Instead he stared straight out into the audience at Elizabeth. "My life has no meaning without my love," he said in a magnetic voice.

Elizabeth found herself mouthing the words along with him, and she shivered. It was sexy watching Joey direct the play she had written. It was like there was a deep, unspoken understanding between them. Not only were they collaborating on the play, but the dialogue seemed to be written about them. Joey locked eyes with Elizabeth, and she stared back at him wordlessly.

"We're ready back here!" Maria yelled from behind the stage.

With a start Joey turned back to the job at hand, and the spell was broken. "C'mon out," he yelled.

Maria brought out a group of kids and arranged them on the stage. "Ashley and Emily, you stand here in the corner. Jennifer and Aimee, you're stage right. Rupert, Tanya, and Maggie—"

Winston tugged on the rope and let the curtain fall.

When all was quiet backstage, Joey gave Winston the signal. "OK, curtain up," he said.

The curtain rose. Maggie and Tanya stood front stage center.

"Hey, that's my dinner," Maggie cried, grabbing the plate from Tanya.

"You want it, you got it!" Tanya yelled, flinging a bowl of spaghetti at her. Soon a full-fledged food fight ensued. Bananas and grapes flew across the stage. Kids climbed on chairs and hurled pasta across the room. The campers screamed and yelled.

Then Jessica appeared from stage left, an expression

of utter serenity on her face. She looked wounded and tranquil. Holding herself like a queen, Jessica walked calmly through the room, seemingly oblivious to the chaos around her.

Suddenly a banana whacked her in the cheek.

"Hey!" Jessica yelled, sweeping it off the floor and hurling it back in the direction from which it came.

"Whoa! Cut!" Joey yelled into the megaphone. It looked like he was trying not to smile. Everybody quieted down. "Now listen, guys, you've got to avoid Alexandra at all costs. And Jessica, if something like this happens, you have to ignore it."

Elizabeth felt a rush of love for Joey as she watched him. He was so good-natured. He was a great director. The kids loved him, and he had complete control over the group. The campers didn't listen to him out of fear, but out of respect.

"Let's run through it one more time," Joey said as Winston let the curtain fall. "And Jessica, keep in character."

Jessica nodded, looking slightly abashed. Then she disappeared behind the wings.

"Curtain up!" Joey called again. The curtain rose, and the food fight resumed. Jessica appeared as before and floated serenely across the stage. Joey talked through the megaphone as she reached center stage.

"OK, everybody freeze!" The kids all stood perfectly still, holding their positions like statues. Some had their arms up in the air, as if ready to launch some food, and others stood still in a running stance. Maggie and Tanya were facing each other, their arms on each other's shoulders. One little boy was

154

crouched on the ground as if ready to take off in a race.

"OK, Liz, now you've made your decision," Joey guided her.

"I'm Jessica," Jessica said, a devilish smile on her face.

"Huh? Oh, right, Jessica," Joey said, a flush rising up his neck to his face. He coughed. "Sorry about that."

"Don't worry about it," Jessica said with a wave of her hand. "It happens all the time." She smiled at Elizabeth and winked.

Looking flustered, Joey stared down at the script and studied his notes. His cheeks were pink, and it looked like he was trying to regain his composure. "OK, you're going to run away to be with the, uh, woodsman," Joey continued. "We need to see it all on your face. Torment, a decision, then calm."

Elizabeth smiled to herself. She wondered if it was difficult for Joey to direct her sister since they looked so much alike. He definitely seemed thrown to have Elizabeth in the audience. She felt her spirits rise. Maybe Joey still felt something for her after all.

Jessica stood perfectly still at center stage and lifted her face to the audience. Winston shone the spotlight on her. Her face was a study in emotions. First she appeared to be engaged in an inner struggle. The blood rose to her cheeks, and she looked anguished. Then a light appeared in her eyes and she stood up straighter. Looking as if she were infused with a new sense of calm, she launched into her soliloquy. "In the flicker of an instant, my fate will be sealed. . . ."

"Great! Terrific!" Joey said when she had finished. "Jessica, you're a natural."

Jessica gave him a charming smile, the dimple in her left cheek deepening.

"OK, now I want the stage cleared," Joey directed. "Next scene is Alexandra alone in the forest. Jessica, take position in the wings stage left."

Joey hopped up on the stage and gathered the chattering kids around. "You guys were great," he said. "That was the best food fight I've ever seen. Now, as soon as the curtain falls, you have to exit stage left in complete silence. Got it?" The group nodded.

"OK, Winston, you can pull the curtain," Joey instructed, jumping off the stage.

The curtain fell and the quiet scampering of feet could be heard.

"Curtain up!" Joey yelled. "Jessica, you're running in the forest, making your escape."

Jessica appeared from behind the curtain and dashed across the stage, a haunted look on her face. She looked scared but determined. She disappeared into the wings on the other side, then came back out a moment later.

"The expression's good, but you've got to slow down the movement," Joey said. "We want to evoke a sense of duration. You're not running from point $A$ to $B$, but you're making your way through a vast, tangled forest."

Jessica frowned. "How can I run without running?"

"Act like you're running in slow motion, or if it makes it easier, pretend you're running underwater," Joey explained. "You're going as fast as you can, but the weight of the water is hindering your speed."

Jessica nodded and Winston let the curtain fall. As the curtain rose Jessica ran in slow motion across the stage, looking tired and anxious. Elizabeth was impressed. It really captured the effect of running long distance.

"Perfect," Joey said quietly as she disappeared in the wings on the other side. But again he directed his gaze toward Elizabeth. A thrill coursed down her spine.

"Really?" Jessica asked, popping her head out again. "I felt completely ridiculous."

"But you *looked* fabulous," Joey said, jumping up onstage. "That's it for the night," he announced. "Let's wrap it up." He patted the shoulders of the extras as they passed by. "Good job, guys," he said.

Maria came down the aisle and sat down next to Elizabeth. "So, what do you think of the production?" she asked.

"Oh, it's great," Elizabeth said, not taking her eyes off Joey. Actually she hadn't really thought about the quality of the play—even though she'd written it. She had only noticed Joey.

Then Joey jumped off the stage and walked down the aisle. The blood rushed to Elizabeth's face. It looked like he was headed straight for her.

But suddenly Nicole materialized out of the wings and ran down the steps. Linking arms with him, she began chattering and led him away.

Elizabeth jumped up, feeling like a knife was wrenching her heart. *What am I doing here, torturing myself?* she wondered. Joey was Nicole's boyfriend, not hers. She had to get that fact through her head. Her time would be better spent writing a romantic letter to Todd.

"Listen, Maria, I'm going to take off. I don't think getting involved in the play is the best idea at this point," she said.

"I think you're right," Maria agreed, her tone sympathetic. "I guess this wasn't such a good idea." She put a hand on Elizabeth's shoulder. "If you need to talk, you know I'm here, right?"

Elizabeth nodded. "I know," she said appreciatively. "See you later." She swung her bag over her shoulder and hurried down the aisle. At least she had Maria. When she reached the door, she turned back and waved. Maria waved back, her deep brown eyes full of concern.

Monday afternoon after his tumbling workshop Winston limped to the stables. Everything hurt. His thighs were tight, his rear ached, and his back was screaming in agony. He had been worthless in the tumbling workshop. All he could do was point. Now he was even walking like a cowboy, with his legs about a foot apart from each other. One of the boys had said, "Hey, Winston, you look like you've been sleeping on a horse."

Even though he could barely walk, Winston was determined to master horseback riding. After his first fall he had managed to stay up on Silkwood for the entire afternoon. As long as he remained seated firmly in the saddle and held the reins lightly, it was no problem. After a few hours he had begun to get the hang of it.

Winston ambled into the stable to find Sky raking a pile of manure.

"Hey, Sky," Winston said.

Sky looked up and stood his rake in the ground. "How you doing, Winston?" he asked. "You looked pretty good out there yesterday."

Winston grinned proudly. "I think I'm catching on."

"Do you want to take her out again?" Sky asked.

Winston nodded.

"Be right with you," Sky said, sticking his rake into the pile of manure. He threw the rest of the pile out of the stable and dropped the rake on the ground. Then he disappeared into the wood building.

A few minutes later Sky brought Silkwood out of the stables. She whinnied and nosed Winston gently as if she recognized him.

"That's a girl," Winston said, patting her shiny flank.

Putting one foot in the stirrup, Winston hopped up on Silkwood like a pro.

Sky grinned, his blue eyes crinkling in his tanned face. "Soon you'll be taking her to horse races," he said.

Winston lifted his hat to Sky. "See you at the race-track!" he called. Then he clicked his heels against the horse's sides and pulled lightly on the reins. "Giddyup!" he commanded.

Silkwood took off at a brisk trot and headed for

the plains. Holding the reins lightly, Winston took in his surroundings with a sense of awe. It was a beautiful clear afternoon, and the scent of flowers filled the air. Lush green hills stretched out ahead of him, and a sparkling brook gurgled to his right.

Winston gently pressed the left rein against Silkwood's neck and directed her to a meadow overgrown with wildflowers. She turned and pranced along happily. The lavish greenery and the lulling rhythm of Silkwood's trot infused Winston with a sense of calm and well-being.

As they rode across the meadow Winston smiled to himself. He was beginning to feel proud of himself. He had never thought he would find himself on the back of a horse. *Enjoying* it. He sat back comfortably in the saddle and pulled his hat low over his forehead.

"Hey, cowboy!" a familiar voice yelled. Winston twisted around in the saddle in the direction of the voice.

It was Lara. Winston almost fell off the horse when he saw her. Lara was leaning against a tree at the edge of the meadow, and she was looking particularly sexy. She was wearing hip-hugging jean shorts and a mint green crop top. Her white midriff was exposed, and her hair was swinging up on her head in a flippy tail.

Regaining his composure, Winston waved and steered the horse around. "Let's go, Silkwood," he said. The horse lifted her head in the air and trotted across the plains back to the stables. Pulling on the reins, Winston brought the horse to a stop near Lara.

"Hi, Lara," Winston said, feeling suddenly shy.

"Aaron said I could find you here," Lara said in a flirtatious tone.

"Yeah, well, I've just been galloping across the plains with Silkwood here," Winston said.

"Mind if I join you?" Lara asked, hooking a foot in the saddle and jumping up brazenly.

"Uh . . . sure," Winston agreed nervously, even though it was a moot point. He swallowed hard. Lara was sitting about six inches in front of him and her body was turned facing his.

"So how's Maria?" Lara asked.

"Same old thing," Winston said. His voice cracked as he answered. He wasn't used to all this attention. And particularly coming from a beautiful girl sitting inches away from him on a horse.

Suddenly Lara lifted her face to his and caught his lips in hers, kissing him fervently. He felt powerless to stop her. But after a few breathless moments he pushed her away.

"Lara, we can't do this," he said. "You know our dating is against the rules. And I still have a girlfriend."

Lara laughed bitterly. "Some girlfriend," she said.

She brushed his lips one more time and hopped off the horse. "You'll come around," she said confidently. Winston gulped as he watched her sashay away.

# Chapter 12

"Now, everybody has to finish their hoagies before dessert," Tanya said in a stern voice at lunch on Tuesday. "You all need your energy for dance class later on today."

Tanya was sitting at the head of the table, playing Jessica for the day. She was wearing a pretty floral split skirt and her purple sweatshirt. She had painted her nails pink and was wearing matching lipstick. Her hair was loose around her shoulders, and she had a purple bow in it.

Jessica was relieved that Tanya had all the girls' attention. She was in a bad mood and didn't feel like dealing with the Wannabees. Lacey had been giving her dirty looks all day, and Jessica still hadn't heard from Paul. She'd thought for sure he would have called or written by now.

Tanya flipped her hair back over her shoulder and batted her eyelashes at the campers. "I have the starring role in the play and all the guys love me. Especially Derek, my leading man." Tanya sighed and flicked her wrist in a sophisticated gesture. "But he's too old for me."

The girls giggled. Tanya's imitation of Jessica was so comic that even Jessica had to laugh.

Sofia's hand shot up.

"Yes, Sofia, do you have a question?" Tanya asked.

"Jessica, what's your favorite color?" Sofia asked.

"Purple!" Tanya shouted out. Then she folded her hands in front of her and looked at the girls. "Now, if everybody has finished their meal, you can all start eating your tapioca pudding."

The girls pushed away their trays and started in on their pudding. Jessica watched in shock as the girls quietly ate their dessert. It looked like Tanya had a better handle on discipline than she did.

Stephanie took one bite of her pudding, then she dropped her spoon in her bowl and pushed it away from her. Sliding off her chair, she ran over to Jessica. "Can I please play you next, Jessica?" she asked politely.

"Well—" Jessica hesitated. She didn't know if it was a good idea to surrender all her authority to the girls.

"Pwitty please?" Stephanie asked, her big green eyes pleading.

Jessica could feel herself softening. But before she could answer, Sarah had taken her place on Jessica's other side. "I want to play you next!" she announced, her arms folded stubbornly across her chest.

Then all the kids hopped up and surrounded Jessica, each begging to be her for a day. "Me next! Me next!" they all clamored together, jumping all over her. Soon they were all fighting and pushing each other, screaming, "I'm next! I'm next!"

"Everybody quiet down!" Jessica said, trying to restore order.

"Everybody quiet down!" Stephanie repeated.

"Who said you could be Jessica?" Sarah asked in indignation.

"I'll be her if I want to," Stephanie insisted. "I asked first!" She swept out an arm and pointed to herself, knocking over a cup of bug juice in the process. The red liquid spilled over the table onto Sarah's dress.

"Hey! You got your drink on my dress!" Sarah yelled. She picked up the remains of her hoagie and threw it in Stephanie's mop of frizzy red hair.

"Yuck!" Stephanie wailed, wiping bread and cheese from her hair. Reaching across the table, she grabbed her dish of tapioca pudding and aimed for Sarah. "You asked for it," she yelled, letting the pudding fly. Sarah ducked and the pudding hit Maggie in the face.

"Food fight!" Maggie yelled with glee. She wiped her face on her sleeve and reached for a bunch of pickle slices on her tray.

Maggie threw her pickles at Anastasia, and Anastasia rebounded with a slice of onion. Soon it was all-out war. Lettuce and tomatoes showered the benches, pickles shot across the table, and tapioca pudding flew through the air.

Jessica climbed up on a bench. "Stop it!" she yelled at the top of her lungs.

"Stop it! Stop it!" the kids shouted, imitating her. A bowl of pudding went whizzing by Jessica's head and clattered onto the floor.

Jessica looked at the chaos in alarm. It seemed like she had started a revolution.

Suddenly Lacey appeared, her face purple with fury. "What in the world is going on here?" she demanded.

The kids immediately settled down and jumped into their seats, starting to giggle.

"U-uh, well—," Jessica stammered, stepping down quickly onto the floor. A tomato dropped from her hair onto the table.

"I don't know what has come over you, but you had better pull yourself together and fast," Lacey declared, her hands on her hips. She gave Jessica a pointed look and lowered her voice. "One more problem from you, young lady, and you're gone. Do I make myself clear?"

Jessica nodded and gulped. "Crystal clear," she said.

Lacey turned and marched away.

"Crystal clear!" the campers sang out.

"Elizabeth! Over here!" Maria called as Elizabeth entered the lounge of the lodge Tuesday evening. In the mess hall Lacey had announced that all counselors were to attend a staff meeting after dinner.

Elizabeth waved, but she hesitated before sitting down. She quickly scanned the room, looking for

Nicole and Joey. After her experience at play practice she had vowed to avoid them. There was no point in inflicting any more self-torture.

The cozy lounge was full, and it looked like everybody was already there. Winston and Aaron were sitting on a couch with their feet propped up on a coffee table, Jessica was lounging on the floor with Lila and Bo, and Angela was curled up in an armchair.

Then Elizabeth caught sight of Nicole and Joey. They were sitting together in a love seat on the far-right side of the room. Maria had strategically taken a place at the other end of the room.

Elizabeth smiled with relief and hurried to join her.

Lacey banged on a pot. "Attention, everybody! The meeting is hereby opened!" she announced.

"She even has her pot with her!" Maria exclaimed. Elizabeth couldn't help laughing.

Lacey shot them a look, and the girls quieted down.

"Good evening, everybody, and thank you for coming," Lacey said.

She looked around and waited for silence. "I have an important announcement to make," Lacey declared. "The all-camp color war is only a week away."

Elizabeth made a face. "That's important?" she whispered to Maria.

Maria laughed, and Lacey stared at them meaningfully.

"The campers need to start preparing for their events immediately," Lacey continued, whipping out

166

a clipboard. She pushed her glasses down her nose and peered at a list. "Events will include the following: a tug of war, a relay race in the lake, an archery contest, a sack race, a hundred-yard dash, a discus throw—"

Elizabeth tuned Lacey out. Lacey had been playing up this event since the beginning of camp, and Elizabeth found it uninteresting. Marathon sports events weren't her thing.

Unable to control herself, Elizabeth stole a look at Nicole and Joey. Joey was sitting straight up in the couch and Nicole was practically draped over him. Her arm was tucked under his and her head rested on his shoulder. Feeling a pang, Elizabeth looked quickly away and turned her attention back to Lacey.

"Teams will be assigned randomly," Lacey was saying. "I myself will choose the names of the two JCs to be the captain of each team."

Lacey leaned over and picked up a hat. "In this hat are the names of all the junior and senior counselors." She smiled at the group. "Congratulations in advance to the lucky winners."

"Get on with it!" Maria groaned.

With a dramatic flourish Lacey picked a name out of the hat. "The captain of the blue team is"—Lacey peered at the piece of paper—"Nicole Banes!" Then Lacey fished another name out of the hat and looked at it closely. "And the captain of the red team is Elizabeth Wakefield!"

Elizabeth groaned. *This can't be happening.* Not only did she have to be a captain in the stupid camp color war, but she had to compete against Nicole

Banes. Elizabeth sighed. She was definitely under a curse this summer.

Elizabeth could feel Nicole's eyes on her. Turning, she shot Nicole a challenging look. Nicole glowered back.

Silence descended upon the room as the girls glared at each other.

"And one last thing," Lacey said in a booming voice. "I expect a fair fight!"

"She'll get a fight, all right," Elizabeth muttered. "But I don't know about *fair*."

As soon as the meeting adjourned Jessica flew out of the lodge and headed for the phones up the road. She had to get through to Paul. She still hadn't heard from him. She had tried to call him all day from the phone in the lodge, but Lacey had always seemed to be standing near the telephone.

But Jessica knew there was a phone booth about a mile up the road. She had passed it the other night on her way back from Paul's restaurant.

Jessica made her way across the parking lot, crossed the street, and turned onto a dirt path. She began to jog at a steady pace. Beads of perspiration stood out on her forehead, and Jessica panted for breath as she made her way along the path. The up-hill climb was tough.

As she followed the bend in the road the red phone booth came in sight. *Finally,* Jessica thought. Out of breath, she jogged across the street.

Then she stopped short. Lacey was sitting on the bench next to the phone, darning a sweater on her lap. Jessica's mouth dropped open. How did she get there so fast?

"Good evening, Jessica," Lacey said with a smile.

Jessica forced a smile. "Hi, Lacey," she said.

"If you wanted to use the phone, go ahead," Lacey said, her dark blue eyes glittering knowingly. "I'm just waiting for a call."

Jessica jogged in place. "Oh, no. I'm just getting a little exercise." She turned and jogged away. "Nice night for a run!" Jessica waved and continued to jog up the path.

At the top of the hill Jessica stopped, panting for breath. Frustrated, she cut into the forest. She felt trapped.

"Summer camp is supposed to be fun," she muttered to herself as she plodded down the hill back to camp. "Not some kind of prison ward."

# Chapter 13

"Lila, I've gotta talk to you," Jessica said, catching her best friend on her way out of the arts and crafts workshop on Wednesday afternoon. A group of fifteen-year-old girls came streaming out of the cabin behind her.

"What's up, Jess?" Lila asked.

"I need—," Jessica began, but suddenly Lila was surrounded by a group of campers.

"Lila, look how nice this turned out," said a funky-looking girl with spiky red hair and an earring in her nose. She held up a long cord with jade beads on it.

"You were right about the crystal inlay," said another girl, showing Lila a sparkling brooch.

"Oh, that's beautiful," Lila said, fingering the ornate pin.

Jessica waited impatiently while Lila dealt with the campers. Jessica was planning to go see Paul, and she needed Lila to cover for her. She still hadn't received word from Paul, and her heart wrenched at the idea of him not showing up for the play.

The only problem was that she didn't know how to get to him. She couldn't "borrow" Lacey's car in broad daylight. And it was much too far to walk. But she had to get to the restaurant—somehow.

"So, are you in another love bind?" Lila asked, joining her as the campers walked away.

"Well, you could say that," Jessica said. "I've got to see Paul, and I need you to cover for me."

Lila groaned. "Not again. Can't you wait until tonight?"

Jessica shook her head. "I want Paul to come to the play tonight, and I've got to talk to him before then. I sent him a letter with the information, but I haven't heard from him yet. I need to find out what's going on."

"How are you planning to get to the restaurant?" Lila asked.

"That's just the problem," Jessica said. "I have no idea. I can't take Lacey's car in the middle of the day, and she almost busted me the other night anyway."

"Hmm," Lila said thoughtfully. "Do any of the senior counselors have cars here?"

"The only one I know of is Joey, and there's no way he would agree to take me," Jessica said. "And even if he would, he won't have time. He'll be busy with the play all afternoon."

"I guess you'll have to take a long bike ride, then," Lila said lightly.

"A bike! That's a great idea," Jessica exclaimed. She took her friend by the elbow and steered her in the direction of the lodge. She knew there were a couple of old bikes in the rec room.

Lila looked at her as if she were crazy. "Jessica, I was kidding," she said.

"Well, I'm not," Jessica said. She took Lila's wrist and looked at her watch. It was five o'clock. If she hurried, she could make it to the restaurant and back before the play began.

Jessica swung through the doors of the lodge and led Lila to the rec room. A couple of rickety bicycles were leaning against the wall. Jessica grabbed hold of a rusty old orange bike and steered it out the door.

Lila shook her head and followed behind with a sigh. "Jessica, you'll never make it on that thing," she warned. "It's got to be hours away!"

"Sure I will," Jessica declared, pushing through the doors of the lodge and wheeling the bike down the drive. "All it'll take is a little willpower."

"Well, what am I supposed to say if anybody comes looking for you?" Lila asked, looking worried. "Like Lacey, for instance?"

"Just say that I was nervous and went away to be by myself," Jessica suggested. "Say that I'm doing yoga or something to calm my nerves."

"Maybe I should do yoga to calm *my* nerves," Lila said.

"Don't worry about it, Lila," Jessica said with an encouraging smile. "I'll be back before you know it." Jessica put a foot on the pedal and hopped on the bike. "See you at curtain call!" she said with a wave as she pushed off.

Lila just stood at the roadside, shaking her head.

Turning back to the road, Jessica steered the bike to the right. She braked lightly and coasted down the long hill on the bicycle. A steep hill rose up ahead of her. Jessica pedaled quickly, gaining momentum as she approached the incline. She dipped down at the bottom and shot up the hill. But after a few yards her momentum began to give way. Standing up on the pedals, Jessica struggled up the long, steep incline.

Sweating, Jessica instinctively reached for the gearshift. "Shoot," she muttered as she realized she was riding a no-gear bike. Wiping her brow, she gritted her teeth and pedaled further.

When she reached the top of the hill, she put a foot on the ground and took a rest. The road reached out endlessly in front of her. All she could see was the black tar of the highway and the horizon up ahead. *Is this crazy?* she wondered. *Should I just give up now?* Then her determination to see Paul spurred her on. She pushed off the ground and started pedaling.

Winston hurried out of the cabin after tumbling workshop. He had rushed to get dressed so he would beat the boys out of the cabin. He wanted a few minutes to himself to read his mail. He'd received two letters that day at mail call. One was from Maria, and the other was from Lara. He'd been carrying them around with him since lunch, but he hadn't had a moment of privacy.

Winston's stomach coiled as he weighed Maria's letter in his hand. It was heavy. He was sure this letter was Maria's last—a "Dear John" letter. She probably wanted to give him a long drawn-out explanation for breaking up with him.

Winston walked down to the lakeside to read the letters in private. As he made his way across the lawn he mentally prepared himself. There was no reason to get upset. He had been expecting this all along. Just because Maria was interested in someone else now didn't mean he couldn't win her back later.

Winston cracked his lasso in the air, trying to bolster his self-confidence. Then he broke off a piece of grass and twirled it around in his mouth.

Reaching the lakefront, Winston fell down in a patch of sand and dropped the letters at his side. He decided to read Lara's letter first to steel him against the pain of Maria's. *To My Cowboy* was written on the envelope.

*Dear Winston,*
*I've had a crush on you since the first day I saw you in the auditorium doing your hilarious imitation of Lacey.*

Winston's face flamed as he read Lara's gushy note.

*You're the funniest guy I've ever met. Even when you're acting like a cowboy, your goofiness and tenderness never go away— and that's what's so special about you.*

*Thanks for letting me be your assistant in the play. You lit my heart on fire.*

> *Love,*
> *Lara*

Winston folded up the note, feeling flattered. Nobody had ever written him a love letter before. His ego had taken a beating lately, and it was reassuring to know that someone found him desirable. Lara was an extremely attractive girl. Lots of guys would jump at the chance to go out with her. *But* I'm *the one she wants,* Winston reminded himself proudly, basking in the glory of the thought.

*But do I want* her? he wondered suddenly. Doodling with a stick in the sand, Winston tried to work out his feelings for Lara. She was pretty, she was flirtatious, and she was a lot of fun. And she left him cold.

Winston leaned back on his elbows and gazed out at the lake. Suddenly a lot of things became clear to him. He realized that his confusion over Lara was just that—confusion. He had simply been flattered by all her attention. But that was no reason to get involved with her. Lara was much too young for him. Even though she was already fifteen, a year's difference in age could mean a lot.

Most important, he was still head over heels in love with Maria. He didn't want a new relationship. As tempting as it would be to drown his sorrows in Lara, the romance just wouldn't be right. Plus if Lacey found out he was dating a camper, she'd send him home.

Winston made a firm decision to talk to Lara the next chance he got. She must be eagerly waiting for his response, and it wasn't fair to keep her hanging. He just hoped Lara wouldn't take his rejection too hard.

Winston unfolded the note and skimmed it again. Lara was interested in him because he was goofy and tender—not because he was cool and macho. She liked him in spite of the fact that he had become a cowboy. She liked him for himself.

*And so do I,* Winston realized. He liked being who he was. He liked being the class clown. He liked being silly and making people laugh. If Maria wanted a cowboy, then Winston was the wrong guy for her. He could never be a real cowboy anyway. He would always fall off the horse and trip on the lasso.

Feeling a sense of newfound freedom, Winston yanked the bandanna off his neck and flung his lasso far across the sand. Whipping off his cowboy hat, he whirled it in the same direction. Then he wriggled out of his boots and tossed them on the pile.

"Ah, that's better," Winston said with a smile, wriggling his toes. Then he picked up Maria's letter and ripped it open. "Time to face the music," he said.

Fearing the worst, Winston read through the letter quickly. His heart nose-dived into the sand as he skimmed the contents.

*Dear Winston,*
 *My horseback riding skills are getting better and better. . . . Hank and I go out every*

*day. . . . Now I can even ride bareback. . . .*
*I'm going to the country for a few days with*
*my grandmother and Hank, so I won't be able*
*to write.*

*Maria*

Winston winced. Now she was running away with Hank. He just couldn't understand why she wouldn't be more direct about it. *I've had it,* he decided. *I'm sick of not being appreciated. I'm going to write her a letter and break up with her myself.*

He picked up the envelope to stuff the letter back in, but a picture fluttered out and fell in the sand. Winston looked at it in alarm. What if it was a wedding shot? *Relax, man,* he told himself. *Don't go jumping to crazy conclusions.* After all, Maria was only sixteen. She wasn't getting married anytime soon.

Winston picked up the picture cautiously and brushed the sand off it. He stared at the image, and his eyes almost popped out of his head. Thinking his imagination was playing tricks on him, Winston closed his eyes and looked again. Then he fell back in the sand and laughed and laughed. The picture was of Maria and an old man in a cowboy hat and chaps. The man had a weathered face and light blue eyes. Winston turned the photo over. *Me and Hank* was written on the back.

Winston was flooded with relief. He couldn't believe he had ever doubted Maria. Or himself. Most of all, he couldn't wait to tell her all about it. He knew she'd have a good laugh.

❖　　　❖　　　❖

An hour later Jessica stood up on the pedals of her bicycle, struggling to make it through the last stretch on the two-lane highway in town. She breathed a sigh of relief as she caught sight of the blinking neon light of the restaurant ahead. Braking slightly, she coasted down the road. Her whole body was screaming out in agony. Her lips were parched, and her body was drenched in sweat.

As she reached the restaurant she wiped a hand on her brow and steered the bike into the parking lot. She slid off the bike and pushed down the kickstand with her foot. Her body trembled from heat and exhaustion.

Crossing the lot, Jessica swung through the door of the restaurant. She knew she looked like a wreck, but at this point she didn't care.

The restaurant was almost deserted. A few customers sat at the tables, drinking coffee and reading the newspaper. One of the regulars was perched on a stool. But it looked like nobody was working behind the counter. Jessica hopped up on a stool and waited.

Then a waiter came out of the kitchen, holding a tray in his hand. He was a young guy wearing black pants and a white shirt. He had long, dirty blond hair pulled back in a ponytail and a tiny gold hoop in his left ear.

He set a plate down in front of the man at the counter and turned to Jessica. "Can I help you?" he asked.

"Yeah, can I have a drink of water?" Jessica asked.

"Sure," he said. "Coming right up." Moments later he placed a tall glass of ice water in front of her. Jessica drank it down in one gulp and set it on the counter.

"Thanks," she said, sliding off the stool.

The waiter laughed. "Is that all you wanted?"

"Actually I'm looking for Paul," Jessica explained. "Is it OK if I go in back?"

"He's not here," the waiter said.

"What do you mean, he's not here?" Jessica asked.

"Wednesday is Paul's day off," the waiter explained.

Jessica collapsed into a booth. She had come all this way for nothing. Then she sat up with determination. Wherever he was, she'd find him.

"Do you know where he is?" Jessica asked.

"He's probably at home," the waiter replied.

"Can you give me the address?" Jessica asked. "I've got my bike, and I could ride over there. I've got to see him. It's *extremely* important."

The waiter shook his head. "I'd be happy to give you the address, but unfortunately you can't get there by bike. You have to take the highway through a tunnel, and there's no bike path."

Jessica's face fell.

"Tell you what," the waiter said. "I've got a break. Leave your bike here and I'll take you to the Mathises' house in my Jeep."

"Oh, thank you," Jessica said, giving him a grateful smile.

A half an hour later the waiter dropped her off in front of a small white house in a residential area. A rickety old porch led to the front door and a white picket fence surrounded the yard. A little terrier was playing in the grass.

"See you!" Jessica waved, jumping out of the car and hurrying across the lawn.

The dog yapped at Jessica as she moved toward the house.

Jessica put her finger to her lips and the dog abruptly quit barking. "Good dog," she whispered.

Jessica ran up the steps of the porch and lifted her finger to ring the bell. But before she reached the doorbell, the door swung open. Paul stood in the doorway, barefoot and unshaven. He was wearing faded torn blue jeans and a white cotton shirt.

"What are you doing here?" he asked rudely.

"I had to find you," Jessica said.

"Well, I'm busy," Paul said in a curt voice, turning around abruptly and letting the door shut behind him.

Undaunted, Jessica pushed open the door and followed him down the hall to a big yellow kitchen. Pots and pans hung on the wall, and fresh orange tulips stood in a vase on a butcher-block table.

Paul wheeled around when he heard her footsteps. "I told you, I'm *busy*. Now would you mind getting out of my house?"

Jessica shrugged out of her backpack and rubbed her aching neck. "Would you just hear me out?" she asked.

"No, I won't," Paul responded, his arms folded across his chest. "I don't want to hear any more false promises from you. I already told you what I think about dumb blondes. And you haven't exactly shown me that you're any different from the rest of them."

Jessica could feel her blood boiling. If there was one thing she couldn't take, it was being called a dumb blonde. "Fine, have it your way," she said, her face set. "I'm sorry I sent you the letter in the first place." She grabbed her backpack and stormed down the hall.

Paul ran down the hall after her and yanked her around by the arm. "What letter?" he demanded.

"The letter I sent you explaining that I couldn't come Monday night," Jessica said, tapping her foot impatiently. "Lacey almost caught me and gave me a major lecture."

Paul's face softened. "I never got the letter," he said.

"Well, *good*," Jessica said, still burned up by his attitude. "Now if you wouldn't mind letting go of me, I've got a play to perform."

Paul looked at her intently. "Jessica, I'm sorry. I didn't realize you'd tried to get in touch with me. And I shouldn't have doubted you in the first place."

Jessica tried to look stern, but she could feel her anger fading away. "OK, I forgive you this time," she said, a smile playing on her lips. She waggled a finger at him. "But if I hear one more dumb-blonde comment out of you—"

"Never again, I promise," Paul said, dropping an arm around her shoulders and steering her down the hall. When they walked back into the kitchen, he pulled her into a bear hug. "Oh, Jess, I've got to learn to trust you," he whispered into her hair.

"Yes, you do," Jessica agreed softly. "Because I don't feel like taking any more long bike rides."

Paul pulled back and looked at her in astonishment. "You came on your bike?"

"Well, I only got as far as the restaurant," Jessica said. "A waiter drove me over."

Paul shook his head. "You are really something, Jessica Wakefield."

"That's right," Jessica said, her blue-green eyes sparkling happily. "And don't you forget it!"

"I won't," Paul murmured, pulling her close and bringing his lips to hers. Jessica closed her eyes, lost in his embrace. All she could hear was the whirring of water in the dishwasher and the ticking of the wooden clock in the foyer.

Suddenly the ticking penetrated into Jessica's consciousness. The time! Jessica pulled out of Paul's arms and looked at the clock on the wall. It was after six. She had to get back to the camp—immediately.

"Paul, I've got to get back!" Jessica exclaimed. "The play starts in two hours. In my letter I sent you an invitation to the play. Do you want to come with me now?"

Paul frowned. "My parents have my truck. They're out of town until tomorrow, attending a restaurant conference."

"And my bike is at the restaurant," Jessica said slowly.

Her heart began pounding slowly as reality dawned.

"Paul, is there any way to get to the restaurant?" Jessica asked, her voice rising in panic. "A bus or a train?"

Paul shook his head. "I'm afraid not."

Jessica's heart dropped. *I'm stuck!* she thought.

She bit her lip as she contemplated the situation. Because it was such a small production, they didn't have understudies. And they couldn't reschedule the play for another night. All the kids' parents were coming, as well as important people in the movie business.

Well, there was only one solution. Elizabeth would have to fill in for her. Jessica just prayed that her twin would come to the same realization. Otherwise she was dead.

"Oh, well, let's go outside and look at the stars," Jessica said.

"But what about the play?" Paul asked.

"I'm going to have to worry about all that later," Jessica said with a smile. "Right now I've got more important things on my mind."

"Like what?" Paul asked.

"Like you," Jessica responded. Paul took her hand and led her outside.

"Lila, what are you doing here?" Elizabeth asked in surprise at the drama cabin on Wednesday. She had come backstage looking for Jessica. She wanted to wish her sister good luck, but she couldn't seem to find her anywhere. She had stopped by the JC cabin, but Jessica wasn't there. And it looked like she wasn't in the drama cabin either.

Lila glanced up, a needle in her mouth. A little girl stood in front of her in a long dress, fidgeting impatiently while Lila adjusted the hem of the costume.

183

Lila took the needle out of her mouth. "Joey asked me to help out with last-minute art direction before the play," she explained.

Elizabeth's mouth dropped open. "You can sew?" she asked in astonishment.

Lila snorted. "Of course I can sew," she said with a toss of her hair. "I took a basic fashion design course at the Sweet Valley Art Academy when I was going out with Robby."

"Oh, sorry, I didn't mean to insult you," Elizabeth said quickly. "You just don't seem the type to, you know, work with your hands a lot."

*That didn't come out right.* Elizabeth hurried on. "I mean, I'm just surprised to see you on this end of the fashion industry. Usually other people design *your* clothes for you." Elizabeth bit her lip. She didn't think she was making this any better.

Lila looked annoyed. "Elizabeth, did you want something or did you just want to chat about my design skills?"

"Actually I was wondering if you've seen Jessica," Elizabeth said.

Lila looked down and shifted her feet. "Uh, I think she said she wanted to be by herself for a while. She's got last-minute jitters."

"Do you know where she went?" Elizabeth asked.

Lila shrugged. "She said something about communing with nature."

"Thanks, Lila," Elizabeth said, dashing out of the cabin. She headed for the lakefront. If Jessica wanted to calm down, she was sure to head straight for the water. But when Elizabeth got to the lake, the beach was deserted. Nobody was lying out on the sand, and only a few windsurfers were in the water. She looked in the boathouse and the supply shed. Nobody was there.

*That's funny,* Elizabeth thought, walking in the direction of the activities cabin. She peeked in the door of the dance cabin, thinking Jessica might have gotten caught up in a dancing lesson. But the long mirror reflected back an empty room.

Then Elizabeth quickly checked all the other activities cabins. They were deserted. Elizabeth was beginning to feel concerned. Maybe something had happened to Jessica. Maybe she had taken a boat out alone on the lake and capsized.

Elizabeth felt panic rising in her. Hurrying to the mess hall, she quickly ran through all the rooms, peeking her head into the lounge, the rec room, and the auditorium. Jessica wasn't in any of those places. Then she dashed back to the drama cabin. Something was wrong. She could feel it in her bones.

A flurry of activity greeted her as she pulled open the door. Stage managers were running around fitting costumes and putting on makeup. Actors were walking around reciting their lines. The stage crew was setting up scenery on the stage, pounding in nails and adjusting the lighting.

Elizabeth hurried up to Lila and Maria, who were sifting through costumes in the wardrobe closet. "Jessica's nowhere to be found," she announced. "I've searched the entire camp. I can't understand it."

"I think I can," Lila said with a sigh.

"Oh, no!" Elizabeth exclaimed. "Jessica's up to something, isn't she?"

Lila nodded, a guilty expression on her face.

Elizabeth put her hands on her hips. "Lila Fowler, did you just send me on a wild goose chase?" she asked angrily.

"I'm sorry, Elizabeth," Lila said. "Jessica made me promise to keep it a secret."

"To keep *what* a secret?" Elizabeth demanded.

"Well, I'm not supposed to say anything, but I guess this is an emergency situation," Lila said, looking around to make sure nobody else could hear them. "You guys promise to keep this totally confidential?"

Maria and Elizabeth nodded. Elizabeth tapped a foot impatiently.

"Jessica's been seeing Paul Mathis, a guy who lives in town," Lila explained. "She sneaked off to see him this afternoon. For some reason she must not be able to get back to camp."

"Nothing ever changes," Maria said. "Jessica's pulling the same tricks she did in junior high."

"How did she get into town?" Elizabeth asked.

Lila sighed. "On a bicycle."

"On a bicycle?" Elizabeth asked, looking at Lila with a stunned expression on her face.

"Don't look at me," Lila said, throwing her hands up in the air. "She's *your* sister."

"Well, it must be love," Maria said.

"I can't believe this!" Elizabeth said, pacing back and forth. She was both worried and infuriated. Jessica could have gotten into an accident or have been abducted on the road. On the other hand, she might have just lost track of the time. After all, Jessica didn't wear a watch, and she wasn't known for

186

being responsible. She was probably just hanging out with Paul in the restaurant, having a good time. Elizabeth was furious. This was one of the stupidest stunts Jessica had ever pulled.

Elizabeth looked at her watch. It was seven o'clock, just an hour before the play. "We've got to borrow a car and find her immediately."

Maria sighed. "Elizabeth, you know that old saying, 'The show must go on'?"

Elizabeth nodded. "Exactly—that's why we've got to find her immediately."

"I don't think we have time," Maria said.

Elizabeth bit her lip. Maria was right. They'd never get to the restaurant and back before the opening.

"It looks like you have no choice," Maria said.

Lila nodded. "Maria's right."

"No choice about what?" Elizabeth cried.

"The twin switch," Lila said.

*"What?"* Elizabeth exclaimed. "You want me to play Jessica's role?"

"Sure, you'd be great," Maria said. "Nobody would be the wiser."

"No way," Elizabeth said, shivering at the idea of getting onstage. "I'm a writer, not an actor. I'm a behind-the-scenes kind of person."

"You wrote the lines of the play. You know them," Lila insisted.

"C'mon, Elizabeth, we need you here," Maria added. "It's our only option. Otherwise we're going to have to cancel the production. All the campers will be crushed. And all their parents—"

Elizabeth stopped her with a wave of her hand. "All right, all right, I'll do it," she said.

"Oh, Liz, thanks! You're a lifesaver!" Maria said, giving her a hug.

*I'll fill in for Jessica now,* Elizabeth thought. *But afterward I'm going to strangle her.*

# Chapter 14

"Summer love is sweet but cruel," Elizabeth intoned in her final monologue of the play on Wednesday evening. "As fleeting as the light of a firefly." The spotlight was on her as she stood in the middle of the stage.

As she spoke, Elizabeth remembered writing those words. She must have unconsciously known that this summer would be tough on her heart. She almost forgot that she was supposed to be acting as she went through the rest of the monologue.

Turning a profile to the audience, she gazed up to the sky and pronounced her final words. "But I am not choosing my fate. It has chosen me."

A tear ran down her face as the curtain fell. The audience burst out in spontaneous applause.

Wiping her cheek, Elizabeth hurried into the wings to find Derek. She and Maria had had to let him in on the twin switch. He would have realized immediately that Alexandra wasn't Jessica. He had promised to keep it top secret, and he had been coaching Elizabeth before each scene.

"Derek, what next?" Elizabeth asked in a stage whisper.

"We're hunting for berries to survive," Derek explained. "You enter stage right, I enter stage left. We meet in the middle, feed each other, kiss, and disappear into the woods."

"Got it," Elizabeth said, rushing around behind the stage to the wings at the other side.

The curtain opened to reveal a tangled, enchanted forest. The campers were dressed up in tree costumes, waving their arms slowly to achieve the effect of wind drifting through their branches. Two white doves swung from wires, and a bright orange moon hung suspended from the ceiling.

Elizabeth and Derek entered the stage opposite each other, plucking berries from the trees. When they reached each other, they linked hands and walked to the front of the stage. After they dropped the berries solemnly in each other's mouth, they kissed to seal their fate. Then they linked hands and drifted backward, disappearing in the sea of trees. The curtain fell.

Moments later the curtain rose again to reveal a black stage. The sounds of chopping wood filled the auditorium.

There was a hush in the audience, and then wild applause broke out.

As the curtain fell for the final time, Elizabeth was flooded with relief. She couldn't believe she had really done it. The play had gone without a hitch. She hadn't been sure of the blocking, but she had remembered all the lines.

"Bravo! Bravo!" the crowd yelled.

The curtain rose again. The audience was on its feet in a standing ovation, yelling and clapping. Elizabeth and Derek linked arms and took a deep bow.

Joey rushed out with a bouquet of roses and placed them in Elizabeth's arms.

"Bravo, Jessica!" the campers screamed.

After the third curtain call Winston let the curtain fall a final time. Then he flicked on the lights of the auditorium, feeling satisfied with himself. The play was over, and his lighting system had worked perfectly. But most important, he didn't have to be a cowboy anymore and he hadn't lost Maria. Now he just had to deal with Lara.

Winston ducked under the curtain to find a forest of trees hugging and congratulating one another. Weaving through the trees, Winston crossed the stage to the other side, where Lara was working the lights. She was sitting on a stool with the remote control, dimming the lights onstage.

"Hi, Winston," Lara said, giving him a bright smile.

"Uh, hi, Lara," Winston said, his voice coming out as a squeak. He pulled up a stool and sat down next to her.

"So, did you get my letter?" she asked flirtatiously.

Winston's face flamed. He was glad it was dark so she couldn't see him blush.

191

"Uh, yeah, that's what I, um, wanted to talk to you about," Winston said.

Lara looked at him expectantly.

"You see, I, well, ah, hmm," Winston began. He coughed and hesitated, trying to figure out how to break the news to her. He wanted to let her down easy. Girls were very vulnerable at her age.

"That's easy for you to say," Lara said with a laugh.

Winston cleared his throat and tried again. "Well, I was thinking, I'm, uh, well, I don't know if—" Winston stopped again, feeling tongue-tied.

"You don't know if *what*?" Lara asked.

Winston took a deep breath and the words came out in a rush. "Lara, I'm sorry, but I just don't think it could work out between us. I'm still in love with Maria, and I think she's still in love with me." He looked at the ground, then peeked up at her, nervous to see her reaction.

"Oh." Lara shrugged, not seeming very concerned. "It's no big deal. I decided that older men aren't that much fun anyway. I want to find someone my own age—someone who isn't so tied down," she said. Lara jumped up. "See you around, Winston!" she said.

As Winston watched, Lara made a beeline for a guy who was working the sound system. He was wearing a baseball cap, and he looked about fourteen years old.

"Hi, Lara!" he said as she approached.

"Need some assistance?" she asked in a flirtatious tone.

Winston sighed and slumped down on the stool. He felt positively middle-aged.

✳    ✳    ✳

192

"Thank you, thank you," Elizabeth said as she ran through a forest of congratulating hands backstage. She charged through the crowd determinedly, a smile fixed on her face.

"Jessica, you were wonderful!" a girl dressed up as a tree called.

"Great performance!" another girl said.

"Thank you," Elizabeth said, feeling as if her face were going to crack from smiling so much.

Elizabeth sighed. She was anxious to get out of the backstage area. She just wanted to get to the dressing room, take off her makeup, and go home. Most of all, she wanted to get away from Joey. He had directed her all evening, and she could feel his presence even when he wasn't around.

Suddenly Joey appeared out of nowhere. "I've got to talk to you," he said in a low, urgent voice. Taking her hand, he pulled her into a dark corner.

Elizabeth could feel her pulse quicken as Joey stood close to her.

"I've been studying you all summer," Joey said. "I knew you had hidden emotions that were waiting to emerge." He took her hands in his and stared deep into her eyes.

Elizabeth felt a stab of pain as she realized that Joey thought he was talking to Jessica, not her. But as his lips came closer to hers, she decided she didn't care.

After a breathless kiss, fresh tears ran down her face. It was too much for her. First Joey was interested in Nicole. Now he was interested in Jessica.

Yanking herself out of his arms, Elizabeth turned

to run away, sobbing. But Joey grabbed onto her arm and spun her around.

"Let go of me," Elizabeth said angrily.

"Why should I?" Joey asked, his voice thick with emotion.

"I'm not Jessica, I'm Elizabeth," she said.

"I know," Joey whispered, pulling her close again.

"You know?" Elizabeth asked, relaxing in his arms.

"I've known the whole time. I recognized you the moment you walked onstage," Joey said. "Do you think I'm stupid? You and Jessica are completely different people—with completely different styles of acting. I'd never mistake you for your sister."

"Well, you did make a slip at play rehearsal," Elizabeth said, smiling between her tears.

"That's because you were distracting me," Joey said with a grin.

Then Joey's expression turned serious. He brushed the tears away from her eyes. "You can't resist this and neither can I, Elizabeth," he said in a soft voice. "Even if our love has to be painful and fleeting, we have to seize the moment and live for today."

"But what about—?" Elizabeth started to protest. Joey pressed a finger to her lips. "We can talk about all the details later. Meet me at midnight at the lake."

"I'll be there," Elizabeth whispered. Joey gave her a brief, searing kiss, then left.

Elizabeth stood in the shadows, her heart pounding.

Just then the curtain behind her rustled. Elizabeth jumped and whirled around.

Nicole stepped out and stood before Elizabeth. "You'll regret that, Wakefield," she said dangerously.

"I've been dreaming of this for days," Joey said as he and Elizabeth drifted in the middle of the lake on a canoe at midnight. He wrapped his arms around her and Elizabeth leaned back against his chest.

"Mmm," Elizabeth murmured, relaxing as the canoe lilted gently in the water. "We're finally getting a chance to finish what we started."

Elizabeth closed her eyes, trying to shut out the world and its trivial problems. She was with Joey, and that was all that mattered. But a nagging thought kept returning to her. What about Nicole? Wasn't Joey seeing Nicole? Elizabeth pushed the thought away. Joey was with her now. Elizabeth had no right to demand an explanation. After all, she was the one who broke up with him.

"So I guess I owe you an explanation," Joey whispered in her ear.

Elizabeth sat up with a start. "You just read my mind," she said.

"You probably think everything I told you was a lie, that I was interested in Nicole the whole time," Joey said.

"The thought did cross my mind," Elizabeth admitted.

"I don't care for Nicole and I never did," Joey declared. "I was just so hurt and angry that I wanted to hurt you back." He looked abashed. "I'm sorry, Elizabeth. I guess that's pretty petty."

"No. After what I said to you in the cafeteria, I

don't blame you," Elizabeth said. Then she bit her lip. "I'm sorry, too," she said softly. "I shouldn't have said what I said."

"But if that's what you thought you felt, then you had a right to say it," Joey said.

Elizabeth shook her head hard. "It was all a lie. All of it. Nicole blackmailed me. She said if I didn't break up with you, she would tell Todd everything. And I guess I wasn't ready to give Todd up."

Joey swore under his breath. "That deceiving little—"

"Well, it's all in the past now," Elizabeth interrupted him, touching his arm. "I don't care if Todd finds out now. I know that you're the one for me."

"And you're the one for me," Joey said, pulling her into his arms and holding her tight.

But even through the warmth of his arms, Elizabeth felt a chill crawl up her spine. Nicole's words were echoing in her brain. *You'll regret that, Wakefield. . . .*

Elizabeth snuggled even closer to Joey. She had the uneasy feeling that things at camp were about to spin even more wildly out of control.

"Mmm," Jessica said, flipping over in the grass and snuggling close to Paul.

Paul murmured in his sleep and threw an arm over her.

Opening her eyes slowly, Jessica looked up at a midnight blue sky sparkling with twinkling stars. Feeling disoriented, she tried to place herself. Where was she? What time was it? Why was she outside?

Then Jessica bolted up. She was on the lawn in Paul's backyard, and it was the middle of the night. In Montana! They must have fallen asleep looking at the stars.

"Paul, Paul!" Jessica shook him.

"Huh?" Paul said groggily, yawning and opening his eyes.

"We fell asleep!" Jessica exclaimed.

Paul sat up and looked around him. "Uh-oh," he muttered.

"Do you know what time it is?" Jessica asked, panicked.

Paul looked at his watch, then he turned worried eyes to her. "It's after midnight."

"How am I ever going to get back to camp now?" Jessica asked in despair.

Paul shook his head. "I was just wondering the same thing."

Jessica groaned and flopped onto the grass.

For the millionth time in her life, she had to pray for a miracle.

*Maybe Lacey didn't invent that camp legend after all. Maybe there really is a killer roaming the woods surrounding Camp Echo Mountain. Find out in Sweet Valley High #125,* **Camp Killer,** *the third and final book of the SVH gang's sizzling summer camp miniseries. Don't miss it!*

Bantam Books in the Sweet Valley High series
Ask your bookseller for the books you have missed

| #1 | DOUBLE LOVE | #45 | FAMILY SECRETS |
| #2 | SECRETS | #46 | DECISIONS |
| #3 | PLAYING WITH FIRE | #47 | TROUBLEMAKER |
| #4 | POWER PLAY | #48 | SLAM BOOK FEVER |
| #5 | ALL NIGHT LONG | #49 | PLAYING FOR KEEPS |
| #6 | DANGEROUS LOVE | #50 | OUT OF REACH |
| #7 | DEAR SISTER | #51 | AGAINST THE ODDS |
| #8 | HEARTBREAKER | #52 | WHITE LIES |
| #9 | RACING HEARTS | #53 | SECOND CHANCE |
| #10 | WRONG KIND OF GIRL | #54 | TWO-BOY WEEKEND |
| #11 | TOO GOOD TO BE TRUE | #55 | PERFECT SHOT |
| #12 | WHEN LOVE DIES | #56 | LOST AT SEA |
| #13 | KIDNAPPED! | #57 | TEACHER CRUSH |
| #14 | DECEPTIONS | #58 | BROKENHEARTED |
| #15 | PROMISES | #59 | IN LOVE AGAIN |
| #16 | RAGS TO RICHES | #60 | THAT FATAL NIGHT |
| #17 | LOVE LETTERS | #61 | BOY TROUBLE |
| #18 | HEAD OVER HEELS | #62 | WHO'S WHO? |
| #19 | SHOWDOWN | #63 | THE NEW ELIZABETH |
| #20 | CRASH LANDING! | #64 | THE GHOST OF TRICIA MARTIN |
| #21 | RUNAWAY | | |
| #22 | TOO MUCH IN LOVE | #65 | TROUBLE AT HOME |
| #23 | SAY GOODBYE | #66 | WHO'S TO BLAME? |
| #24 | MEMORIES | #67 | THE PARENT PLOT |
| #25 | NOWHERE TO RUN | #68 | THE LOVE BET |
| #26 | HOSTAGE | #69 | FRIEND AGAINST FRIEND |
| #27 | LOVESTRUCK | #70 | MS. QUARTERBACK |
| #28 | ALONE IN THE CROWD | #71 | STARRING JESSICA! |
| #29 | BITTER RIVALS | #72 | ROCK STAR'S GIRL |
| #30 | JEALOUS LIES | #73 | REGINA'S LEGACY |
| #31 | TAKING SIDES | #74 | THE PERFECT GIRL |
| #32 | THE NEW JESSICA | #75 | AMY'S TRUE LOVE |
| #33 | STARTING OVER | #76 | MISS TEEN SWEET VALLEY |
| #34 | FORBIDDEN LOVE | #77 | CHEATING TO WIN |
| #35 | OUT OF CONTROL | #78 | THE DATING GAME |
| #36 | LAST CHANCE | #79 | THE LONG-LOST BROTHER |
| #37 | RUMORS | #80 | THE GIRL THEY BOTH LOVED |
| #38 | LEAVING HOME | #81 | ROSA'S LIE |
| #39 | SECRET ADMIRER | #82 | KIDNAPPED BY THE CULT! |
| #40 | ON THE EDGE | #83 | STEVEN'S BRIDE |
| #41 | OUTCAST | #84 | THE STOLEN DIARY |
| #42 | CAUGHT IN THE MIDDLE | #85 | SOAP STAR |
| #43 | HARD CHOICES | #86 | JESSICA AGAINST BRUCE |
| #44 | PRETENSES | #87 | MY BEST FRIEND'S |

|       | BOYFRIEND                        | #107  | JESSICA'S SECRET LOVE            |
|-------|----------------------------------|-------|----------------------------------|
| #88   | LOVE LETTERS FOR SALE            | #108  | LEFT AT THE ALTAR                |
| #89   | ELIZABETH BETRAYED               | #109  | DOUBLE-CROSSED                   |
| #90   | DON'T GO HOME WITH JOHN          | #110  | DEATH THREAT                     |
| #91   | IN LOVE WITH A PRINCE            | #111  | A DEADLY CHRISTMAS               |
| #92   | SHE'S NOT WHAT SHE SEEMS         |       | (SUPER THRILLER)                 |
| #93   | STEPSISTERS                      | #112  | JESSICA QUITS THE SQUAD          |
| #94   | ARE WE IN LOVE?                  | #113  | THE POM-POM WARS                 |
| #95   | THE MORNING AFTER                | #114  | "V" FOR VICTORY                  |
| #96   | THE ARREST                       | #115  | THE TREASURE OF DEATH            |
| #97   | THE VERDICT                      |       | VALLEY                           |
| #98   | THE WEDDING                      | #116  | NIGHTMARE IN DEATH               |
| #99   | BEWARE THE BABY-SITTER           |       | VALLEY                           |
| #100  | THE EVIL TWIN (MAGNA)            | #117  | JESSICA THE GENIUS               |
| #101  | THE BOYFRIEND WAR                | #118  | COLLEGE WEEKEND                  |
| #102  | ALMOST MARRIED                   | #119  | JESSICA'S OLDER GUY              |
| #103  | OPERATION LOVE MATCH             | #120  | IN LOVE WITH THE ENEMY           |
| #104  | LOVE AND DEATH IN                | #121  | THE HIGH SCHOOL WAR              |
|       | LONDON                           | #122  | A KISS BEFORE DYING              |
| #105  | A DATE WITH A WEREWOLF           | #123  | ELIZABETH'S RIVAL                |
| #106  | BEWARE THE WOLFMAN               | #124  | MEET ME AT MIDNIGHT              |
|       | (SUPER THRILLER)                 |       |                                  |

**SUPER EDITIONS:**
PERFECT SUMMER
SPECIAL CHRISTMAS
SPRING BREAK
MALIBU SUMMER
WINTER CARNIVAL
SPRING FEVER
FALLING FOR LUCAS

**SUPER THRILLERS:**
DOUBLE JEOPARDY
ON THE RUN
NO PLACE TO HIDE
DEADLY SUMMER
MURDER ON THE LINE
BEWARE THE WOLFMAN
A DEADLY CHRISTMAS
MURDER IN PARADISE
A STRANGER IN THE HOUSE
A KILLER ON BOARD

**SUPER STARS:**
LILA'S STORY
BRUCE'S STORY
ENID'S STORY
OLIVIA'S STORY
TODD'S STORY

**MAGNA EDITIONS:**
THE WAKEFIELDS OF
SWEET VALLEY
THE WAKEFIELD LEGACY:
THE UNTOLD STORY
A NIGHT TO REMEMBER
THE EVIL TWIN
ELIZABETH'S SECRET DIARY
JESSICA'S SECRET DIARY
RETURN OF THE EVIL TWIN

## SIGN UP FOR THE SWEET VALLEY HIGH® FAN CLUB!

Hey, girls! Get all the gossip on Sweet Valley High's® most popular teenagers when you join our fantastic Fan Club! As a member, you'll get all of this really cool stuff:

- Membership Card with your own personal Fan Club ID number
- A Sweet Valley High® Secret Treasure Box
- Sweet Valley High® Stationery
- Official Fan Club Pencil (for secret note writing!)
- Three Bookmarks
- A "Members Only" Door Hanger
- Two Skeins of J. & P. Coats® Embroidery Floss with flower barrette instruction leaflet
- Two editions of The Oracle newsletter
- Plus exclusive Sweet Valley High® product offers, special savings, contests, and much more!

Be the first to find out what Jessica & Elizabeth Wakefield are up to by joining the Sweet Valley High® Fan Club for the one-year membership fee of only $6.25 each for U.S. residents, $8.25 for Canadian residents (U.S. currency). Includes shipping & handling.

Send a check or money order (do not send cash) made payable to "Sweet Valley High® Fan Club" along with this form to:

**SWEET VALLEY HIGH® FAN CLUB, BOX 3919-B, SCHAUMBURG, IL 60168-3919**

NAME _____
(Please print clearly)

ADDRESS _____

CITY_____ STATE _____ ZIP _____
(Required)

AGE _____ BIRTHDAY_____ /_____ /_____

Offer good while supplies last. Allow 6-8 weeks after check clearance for delivery. Addresses without ZIP codes cannot be honored. Offer good in USA & Canada only. Void where prohibited by law.
©1993 by Francine Pascal                                          LCI-1383-193